'TWAS THE NIGHT BEFORE

ALSO BY JERRY B. JENKINS

FICTION

Soul Harvest
Nicolae
Tribulation Force
Left Behind
The Deacon's Woman (Stories)
Rookie
The Operative

NONFICTION

Field of Hope (with Brett Butler)
Just As I Am (with Billy Graham)
Nolan Ryan: Miracle Man
Singletary on Singletary (with Mike Singletary)
Fourth and One (with Joe Gibbs)
Out of the Blue (with Orel Hershiser)
Meadowlark (with Meadowlark Lemon)
Sweetness (with Walter Payton)
Bad Henry (with Hank Aaron)
Home Where I Belong (with B. J. Thomas)

'Twas the Night Before

A LOVE STORY

Jerry B. Jenkins

VIKING

VIKING
Published by the Penguin Group
Penguin Putnam, Inc., 375 Hudson Street, New York, New York 10014, U.S.A.
Penguin Books Ltd, 27 Wrights Lane, London W8 5TZ, England
Penguin Books Australia Ltd, Ringwood, Victoria, Australia
Penguin Books Canada Ltd, 10 Alcorn Avenue,
Toronto, Ontario, Canada M4V 3B2
Penguin Books (N.Z.) Ltd, 182–190 Wairau Road, Auckland 10, New Zealand
Penguin India, 210 Chiranjiv Tower, 43 Nehru Place, New Delhi, 11009, India

Penguin Books Ltd, Registered Offices: Harmondsworth, Middlesex, England

First published in 1998 by Viking Penguin, a member of Penguin Putnam Inc.

3   5   7   9   10   8   6   4

Copyright © Jerry B. Jenkins, 1998
All rights reserved

PUBLISHER'S NOTE
This is a work of fiction. Names, characters, places, and incidents either are the
product of the author's imagination or are used fictitiously, and any resemblance
to actual persons, living or dead, events, or locales is entirely coincidental.

LIBRARY OF CONGRESS CATALOGING-IN-PUBLICATION DATA
Jenkins, Jerry B.
'Twas the night before : a love story / Jerry B. Jenkins.
p.   cm.
ISBN 0-670-88176-7
PS3560.E485T93   1998
813'.54—dc21   98-34802

This book is printed on acid-free paper.

Printed in the United States of America
Set in Bembo
DESIGNED BY JAYE ZIMET

To the one who still believes

ACKNOWLEDGMENTS

I'm deeply grateful for the encouragement and patience of Carolyn Carlson, the friendship and loyalty of Rick Christian, and the love and cheerleading of Dianna Jenkins.

'TWAS THE NIGHT BEFORE

ONE

The Unlikely Pair

SNOW SWEET-TALKED ITS way into Chicago in broad daylight the day after Thanksgiving. Huge, splatty flakes conspired to blanket, then cripple the city. By dark Chicago moved in slushy slow motion.

In the back of a cab Tom Douten, thirty-one, took the storm personally—as usual. "Winter officially starts what," he said, "a month from now?"

Surfing to a stop in front of Tribune Tower, the cabbie said, "*My* winter starts the first day I have to wear boots."

Tom overtipped, gathered up the competing *Sun-Times* and his notebook, and stepped into the mess. By the time he settled in to write his column, "Douten,

Thomas," the snow in his hair had melted and was running down his neck.

"Pushin' the deadline again, Tommy boy?" Gary Noyer said on his way out. "Wrapped mine up by three."

Tom told himself not to bite, but he couldn't resist. "Then why are you still here?"

"Getting ahead. Building a cushion."

Tom sighed. "Throw a party. Just don't invite me."

"Jealousy is ugly."

Tom pressed his lips together. "Gary," he said slowly, "if I wrote what passes for your column, I'd be far enough ahead to take a month off."

Noyer slowed. "Your last column was almost late."

"There's another way to say 'almost late,' Gary. It's called 'on time.' "

"Oh, Tom," Noyer called over his shoulder, "I almost forgot. My Columbia Prize arrived today. Peek through my window if you'd like to see what one looks like."

Tom's column was twice as popular as Gary's, but he wouldn't bring that up. He felt sleazy enough having allowed Gary to engage him at all.

Tom tore the pages from his notebook and quickly

read them. He raked them into the trash, entwined his fingers in his lap, and rested his chin on his chest. This column would make his boss growl that Tom was doing little to dispel his reputation as resident cynic. The syndicate would complain, again, that his column was "too Chicago." Broadening the readership hadn't been *his* idea. Tripling his income had been nice, but he hadn't asked for that either. Chicago was his beat, and its underbelly his grist. If readers, or syndicators, wanted something else, there were plenty of places to find it.

The smell of LaShawna Jackson's squalid apartment still lay on his coat; the noise of her children echoed in his mind. He closed his eyes and imagined himself a single mother of four in a small flat on West Madison. With no heat.

Mentally nudging fact and emotion, Tom peeked at the screen and reached for the keys. "If this blizzard depresses you as much as it does me," he began, "put yourself in the place of this year's first caller to the Mayor's Emergency Cold Line. . . ."

NOELLA WRIGHT, THIRTY-TWO, peered out the window of her tiny office at Northwestern University in Evanston. She held her breath at the beauty of the snow. Her car was the one lump under the white covering the parking lot. Noella's colleagues, gone as early as possible every day, hardly ever came in on a no-class day.

Noella loved being in her office. She told herself she didn't teach journalism; she taught students. The more hours she spent in her office, the more contact she enjoyed with them.

The lights in the lot reflected bright as day off the snow and made the diamond sparkle on Noella's left hand. She closed the blinds and warmed at the prospect of seeing Tom soon. They met late on his column deadline days, and he was always in good spirits. Well, better spirits anyway. She would have to be a creative writing teacher to say he was always in good spirits. But she had seen huge changes in him since they had fallen in love. They were an unlikely couple, but she saw something in the depths of his soul she wished everyone could see. Especially Sue Beaker.

Sue was Noella's next-office colleague and self-appointed love counselor, and Noella wished she could talk to her right then. Sue had endured all three of Noella's serious relationships, none of which had resulted in marriage. "And now you up and say yes to your polar opposite," she had said. "Emphasis on *polar*."

Twice divorced and now married to a man twenty years her senior, Sue was, by her own admission, "dying of boredom. I could live vicariously through your impending marriage if it weren't so patently doomed."

"Tom and I will live happily ever after, and you know it," Noella told her.

Sue shook her head. "You say it like you mean it, but you're blind. You're Pollyanna Pureheart. He's Sad Sack. You're his Miss Wright. He's your Mr. Douten. Well, I'm doubtin'. I'm a sucker for a love story. But Noella, really. A half-empty-glass guy with a half-full-glass gal?"

Noella had roared. "You call yourself a feminist and you call me a gal?"

"Okay, I was going for alliteration and couldn't make anything else work."

"Trust me, Sue. I know what I'm doing."

"I don't trust you. I care about you, and you don't know what you're doing."

"Be happy for me."

"You're happy enough for the whole J school faculty."

TOM BEGAN A ferocious self-edit that excised every flabby word. The result was copy so tight that his editors complained he was doing his job *and* theirs.

Tom moseyed through the cavernous *Tribune* offices. He hit the can, guzzled at the water fountain, and returned to his screen with a fresh eye. He envied authors who could set their copy aside for days. Satisfied with the final product, he transmitted it to Walt Mathes and printed it out for safety. He allowed himself a smile at the evening ahead. Noella.

He should call and tell her to get out of the weather and go straight home, but she'd call if she couldn't meet him at Round-the-Clock. If she could get there, she'd get there.

Nothing would keep him away either.

NOELLA ACCEPTED THE escort of the security guard, who also helped brush off her car and waited until she started the engine. She rolled down the window to thank him.

"I'll push if I have to," he said.

"No need, Carl," she said, patting the steering wheel. "Front-wheel drive."

Her late-model Nissan took her off campus, around abandoned cars, and to Sheridan Road, a few blocks from Lake Shore Drive. There she waited in a booth at Round-the-Clock. Rita, the late-night waitress, brought Noella's hot chocolate without being asked and assured her Tom's coffee had been cooking for hours.

Tom pulled out of the *Tribune* parking garage in his decade-old Chevy, alternately accelerating and letting up to keep from fishtailing. He picked his way down Michigan Avenue to the LSD, shivering as his mostly defunct heater acted more like an air conditioner, and spent half an hour trying to stay in a navigable groove.

Noella kept her coat on and her collar up, her hands in her pockets between sips. Her phone would ring if Tom couldn't make it. Still, she found herself looking out the window for the man who had once been merely a teaching tool to her, the writer of a column she had recommended to her students for years.

Shortly after the fall term began more than a year before, Noella had acceded to her students' challenge and tried to get Tom Douten to lecture. Four phone calls got no further than his voice mail ("This is Tom. You know the drill." *Beep*), but only an unequivocal no would dissuade Noella. She E-mailed him, then realized he likely received hundreds more of those than phone messages. During Christmas break she resorted to old-fashioned handwriting on "Noella Wright, Ph.D." stationery, bearing the logo of Northwestern's Medill School of Journalism.

DEAR MR. DOUTEN:

My undergraduate students would enjoy meeting you and gaining insight into your world. As you can imagine, a beat reporter who lands his own syndicated column is a hero to budding journalists. If you could find your way clear to join us for a class, I would do all I could to schedule it at your convenience. I will urge students to be prepared with questions and not embarrass you with star treatment.

I have been a regular reader of your features and your column since you first arrived at the *Tribune* several years ago. A paragraph still echoes in my head: "Would-be writers, if they must study in a structured setting, should insist on teachers who are regularly published—not overeducated theorists. And those teachers should balance every minute of class time with writing assignments—real ones."

I took that to heart. You may have seen my by-line in various periodicals, including in-flight magazines and even the *Chicago Tribune Magazine*. All that to say that I am not just a fan, but that I also agree with you. Though I don't cover "the darker side" that seems your stock-in-trade, I marvel at your ability to mine it for consistently educational and uplifting stories of courage.

I've rambled, and I apologize. Please consider my request and let me know. I shall be happy to reimburse you for expenses and for your time.

Sincerely,
Noella Wright,
Professor of Journalism

Tom hated Chicago winters, though he had never known anything else. His car was drafty; his tires were smooth. His body tensed with the effort to keep moving. But the person waiting for him was Noella.

He had been intrigued in January when she kept

calling. He felt obligated to answer her letter, hoping a compliment would help the medicine go down. He tapped out a reply and printed it out:

DEAR MS. WRIGHT:

I have seen your byline. Your work shows real facility. Sorry, but I have nothing to say to students, especially those who aspire to my "station." Those who seek it don't deserve it. The impact on the reader is "the thing," not how the writing (or the response to it) benefits the writer. Your students are all more educated than I. Tell them to write every day, fear no shut door, and pursue stories that force them to face the worst about themselves. All other questions can be answered yes, no, maybe, sometimes, and yes, if you work hard and apply yourself.

Sincerely,
Tom D.

Not even that had put off Noella. She wrote again with "one last attempt to persuade you." He answered with a pleasant but firm no, yet decided to check her out anyway.

Tom rarely ventured farther north than his own

place on LaSalle. North meant privilege and insulation. He couldn't imagine his kinds of stories behind the high-rise windows on the LSD or past the manicured lawns of the North Shore. But an ivory tower prof who wouldn't take no for an answer—while not worth a column—was worth at least a morning. Was it possible she taught the way he would if he believed writing could be taught?

The next free morning he drove to Medill, located Dr. Wright's class, and sat in the back. Tom was not worried about being recognized. The head shot on his column was old, and he dressed like a student anyway, a White Sox cap pulled low over his eyes.

Tom refused interviews and speaking invitations, so he was rarely recognized on the street. Plain was his theme, not so much by design as by neglect. Colleagues accused him of affectation—dressing down—pretending to be a neighborhood guy even after reaching the pinnacle of his profession. To Tom, affectation was a rival columnist's being driven to work in a limousine while writing blue-collar stories. Tom would not live high when the people he wrote about could eat for a year on a week of his pay. Flaunting wealth was so abhorrent to him that he had given away an expensive gift watch rather than appear to have bought it.

Tom was content with his watch, a fifteen-dollar drugstore model with a digital readout and a band made of rubber. He also wore sensible shoes, comfortable pants, print shirts, and he got a "normal" haircut once a month. Gary Noyer had an opinion on that: "Too short for a week and a half, nondescript for a week, then too long for another week and a half."

Tom preferred invisibility. He enjoyed a readership far wider than he believed he deserved. His words could do his talking.

Dr. Wright had her back to the small group of students when Tom sat down. When she turned and stared, everyone else did too.

"Are you lost?" she asked.

"Can't argue with that," he said. "May I just observe?"

"This is Advanced Journalism—"

"May I, or not?" he asked.

She did not respond, so he stayed.

NOELLA OFTEN THOUGHT of that day she had first seen him. Her classes were small and intense, not auditing-friendly. Prospective students were cleared in advance.

So who was this? The cap hid most of his face, but the rest of him looked shabbily handsome in an academic way. He didn't appear to be a security risk, but who knew? She planned to ask him after class with plenty of students still around. But he disappeared.

TOM WAS RELIEVED to see Noella's car at Round-the-Clock. As he trudged through the snow, she smiled at him from the window, and he felt like a different person. He couldn't suppress a smile.

"Rotgut's on its way, lover boy," Rita chirped as she set a midnight breakfast before a CTA driver. Tom nodded his thanks.

He had never been big on public displays of affection, but that didn't stop Noella. Demure and discreet with him at first, she now made her feelings plain. She appeared so thrilled to see him that he felt as if she had cast a spotlight on him and everyone had turned to watch.

He put a hand on her shoulder and leaned in for a peck, but she would have none of it. She reached for him with both hands. "Hi, sweetheart," she said, pulling his face to hers and kissing him hard. To anyone else it looked like a quick greeting, but he got the message when she brushed his lips with her tongue.

He slid into the booth across from her, holding both her hands. Her eyes bored into his. "I love you, you old Scrooge," she said. "You know that, don't you?"

"I know, babe," he said. "Me too."

TWO

The Invitation

NEITHER EVER ORDERED anything to eat so late at night, but Rita didn't seem to mind. Noella appreciated that Tom was unfailingly polite, thanking Rita every time she topped off his coffee. He was also a generous tipper.

Noella had sensed his compassion before she knew him, in the dark features he fashioned for the *Tribune* in his early days as a reporter. His stories had everything. They were cogent, clear, readable, and detailed. "Note the specificity," she told students. "Count the sheer number of facts in the first two paragraphs alone that would require double checking. Clearly, this man's writing—rich and textured as it is—has to take less time than the interviewing, observing, and digging."

She had not lectured about the tenderness between the lines.

"So," she said now, lifting her hot chocolate, "what will Mathes find waiting for him in the morning?"

"Just a piece about the first caller to the Mayor's Cold Line this season."

"I know you've got the copy on you. Let me hear it."

He reached inside his coat. "You really want to hear it? You can read it yourself."

"Humor me," she said.

Back in February she had wept the first time he read her one of his columns—his idea that time. No one could read a piece of writing better than the writer himself. If for some reason he had needed to make it seem her idea each time since, it was worth it.

Tom unfolded the printout and began: "If this blizzard depresses you as much as it does me, put yourself in the place of this year's first caller to the Mayor's Emergency Cold Line. LaShawna Jackson's two-room flat, four-tenths of a mile west of the festive United Center on Madison, is home to her and her four children under seven. . . ."

Tom paused while Rita warmed their drinks, and when he finished, Noella's hands were deep in her pockets, her shoulders hunched against the chill—not

from the restaurant but from the Jackson flat. In just a
few hundred words she had been there. She knew the
woman's name, her situation, her children, their names,
their ages, and something each had said about the snow
and cold—innocent, naive things that made you want
to give them your own parka.

Tom's column included the news that Cold Line
personnel had responded. "Most of us," he concluded,
"have twice the heat, not to mention luxuries, we
need. None of our neighbors should go to bed hungry.
Certainly, none should sleep in the cold."

Noella's chocolate grew cold. "I don't know how
you do it," she managed to say. "I would have written
something about the beautiful snow and the uplifting
season. The tragedy in my story would have been going to a party and being caught away from home in nice
shoes and without boots."

TOM DIDN'T KNOW what to say. He had never learned
to take a compliment. Mathes gave him plenty, but
even Walt occasionally wished Tom would try "one up-
beat piece. Something that warms the reader, makes
him glad to be alive."

"Gag me," Tom had responded. "The sugar flows

so freely out of Noyer's office that it sticks to my shoes."

"Readers love him," Mathes said.

"I'm not in this—"

"—to be loved. Yeah, I know. But when will you cover one too many heinous crimes? When will you not want to get out of bed in the morning?"

Tom wanted to say, "Not as long as there's one more story people need to read," but it sounded cheesy as a greeting card. The truth was, before Noella there *had* been days when he had to talk himself out of bed. Like it or not, he was a realist. He was not convinced that everyone was good, that Norman Rockwell's America still existed (if it ever had), or that those wonderful stories in *Reader's Digest*—nicely written as they were—really represented modern life.

So why was he helplessly and hopelessly drawn to Noella Wright? "I understand it," Gary Noyer had said when another colleague posed the question. "Dr. Wright is your Wayne Newton."

The colleague laughed. Tom did not. "Wayne Newton? Hello?"

"Don't you see?" Gary said. "People who hate schmaltzy Las Vegas acts like Newton's love Wayne Newton anyway. He comes off so sincere, so into it you can't help yourself. He sells it. We hate the other acts because they're phonies and they look like it. He's doing the same act and not that much better, but we believe he loves us and wants to entertain us and that his very happiness depends on pleasing us. So, you find people with happy, optimistic views of life repulsive. Along comes someone who should know better, a modern woman—a communications Ph.D., for the love of all things sacred—but she's so good at Suzy Sunshine even you can't resist her."

Tom prided himself on pithy comebacks but could only respond, "Noyer, you are full of crap."

But was Noyer right? Noella Wright was the type Tom pilloried in print. Yet from that first day in her class he had sensed something genuine in her. He considered himself too good a reporter, too incisive a judge of character to have been hoodwinked.

Tom had noticed Noella trying to get to him after that first class nearly a year before. After disappearing, he knew she would be stunned when he showed up in another class that same day. He owed it to her to introduce himself.

That second class was an eye-opener. Besides being an engaging and demanding teacher, she proved to be a more than capable editor. Noella had made an overhead transparency of the first page of each student's assignment. The class seemed fascinated as she deftly edited each. "This is what editors do," she said, "if you don't do it yourself. The less of this I have to do, the better your grade will be. Learn to do it."

As she quickly made each piece of copy tighter and more readable, students nodded and grunted. "Don't know why I cut that phrase? Look at this. If this is true, do we need that? Why say something twice?"

She was good. She made sense. She edited the way Tom did. He still doubted that writing could be taught, but she sure proved editing could be. And if her editing made the writing better, wasn't she also teaching writing? Maybe he *would* say a few words to her classes, if only to affirm her and urge them to listen.

NOELLA WORRIED ABOUT Tom. he looked tired. He always did after finishing a column. That was one thing she loved so much about him. He worked so hard that he had little left when he was done. He had his diversions. He kept up with two friends from childhood, one an electrician, the other an on-again, off-again carpenter. They weren't impressed with him, he said. That was why they were still friends. When they were to-gether, he liked to tell her, his reputation and income were irrelevant. He and his friends were just three guys from the neighborhood.

Still Noella worried. Did he play enough? His sto-ries were so dark, so often tragic.

"That's real life," he told her. "The rest doesn't mean much."

The day she met him she was surprised by his straightforwardness. She finally reached him as the stu-dents drifted away. "Let me guess," she said. "You're a prospective student, a journalism junkie, or here to tell me I've won the Publishers Clearinghouse Sweepstakes."

"Sorry," he said. "You guessed right this morning. I'm lost."

"Let's see if I can find you," she said. "Start with your name."

"Tom."

"Anything I can help you with, Tom? Medill frowns on drop-ins. It's a security thing."

"I'm an uneducated member of the profession, and I had my doubts whether this stuff could be taught, but I really like the way you teach and the way you edit."

"You write?"

"I'm with the *Tribune*."

"Next you're going to tell me you're Tom Douten."

"Guess I don't need to."

In her letter Noella had promised she would keep her students from treating him like a star, yet she had to keep herself from gushing. She shook his hand and said, "Does this mean you might—"

"If you promise to keep it low-key."

She dropped his hand. "You said no several different ways, yet here you are."

"You wouldn't give up. You reminded me of me."

Noella collected herself and started arranging for his official visit. He turned down any fee or even carfare. "It would cost Medill more for you to fill out the paperwork than to pay me for the mileage. And I'm afraid the mileage would be worth more than my car."

"Your time is worth something," she said.

"I told you my fee. If you can't meet my figure—"

"Gratis?"

"Gratis it is."

THREE

"Forever and . . ."

JUST TEN MONTHS later at Round-the-Clock, Noella sat across from the man who could still banter faster and better with her than anyone she'd ever known. Tom could also make her feel warm all over with just one glance.

When she turned down her collar and unfastened the top button of her coat, Tom reached for her necklace and fingered the pendant. It was a circle, platinum-colored, with the shape of a Christmas tree cut out of it. "Forever and . . ." Tom read quietly.

"Turn it over, hon," she said.

"The back has to say 'a day.' "

Noella smiled. "But it doesn't."

Tom turned the pendant over and red, " 'Born December 24, 1965.' What's this?"

"It's supposed to be my birthday."

"I thought your birthday was December 26," he said.

"I know. Santa got it wrong, that's all."

TOM DOUTEN THOUGHT he had been in love before. Now he sat gazing at Noella across the table, feeling like a fool and not caring.

Gary Noyer had been right in his own obnoxious way. Noella was not Tom's type. But in her he had found everything he had ever wanted without having been aware what that was. She was real. She had character. She loved people. She was sensitive. Okay, so he used to lump such feelings with romance novels and made-for-TV movies.

Yet here he sat, and he wanted to be nowhere else. When he was not with her, his thoughts drifted from her only long enough so he could do his job. Writing had been his life. Now it was a means to an end. His enthusiasm had not flagged, and he would never write only for the money. But the center of his life had become this woman, and he could not articulate why.

Was he worried about growing old alone? Was he tired of playing the cynic? It was no act. Like anyone else, he could point the finger, lay it off on his up-bringing, and make himself the victim. He had learned to trust nothing and no one as surely as if he had majored in Suspicion. With his parents as his professors.

"Seriously," he said, fingering Noella's pendant again, "where'd you get this?"

"I told you. It was from Santa. I was ten."

"You've had it that long?"

Noella smiled, and Tom knew he'd been caught. He often teased her about asking obvious questions. If he said, "I gave Walt a ride to the train," and she asked, "Oh, so you saw him?" Tom would say, "No, I didn't look at him. I just gave him a ride."

"My point"—he tried again—"was that it must be very special to you."

"It's my favorite present. Every December I wear it every day."

"It's not December yet, Noe," he said.

"I know. But if this isn't Christmas weather, I don't know what is."

Tom glanced outside. More snow. How could she love the wet, messy stuff? Knowing it brought her such delight almost made him glad to see it keep coming.

To him, the weather—unless perfect for baseball—was something to complain about.

In spite of himself, Tom watched the snowfall with awe. What made her happy made him happy. He felt a traitor to the negativity cause.

"You know what I would love, Tom?"

"Anything you want, baby."

"But I might take advantage."

"There's nothing I'd like more. What would you love?"

"A walk in the snow."

"Feel free," he said. "Knock yourself out."

"You'd let me walk alone at this hour, wouldn't you?"

"I wouldn't insult your independence by insisting on escorting you."

Noella sighed. "Thomas, you know I'm going to win this one, so why don't you just get your coat on?"

"I'm not even wearing boots."

"I'm not talking about crossing Siberia to the gulag," she said. "We'll stick to cleared sidewalks, and I promise not to keep you out past your bedtime."

It was against his nature to cave. "I'll sweeten the deal," she said. "I'll let you hold my hand. I might even let you put your arm around me."

He sighed. "Lead on."

BEING OPTIMISTIC DIDN'T mean Noella couldn't be bossy at times, but that wasn't why her previous relationships hadn't worked out. She'd liked those guys, each in his own way. But had she loved them? She had told each that she did. She hadn't intended to lie, but down deep she knew better. She enjoyed the attention, the devotion, the fun. But something always eventually nagged her. Noella believed she had a soul mate somewhere. She wasn't sure what that meant or how she would know when she found him. She had broken three hearts, and guilty as she felt about wounding men she cared about, she refused to prolong relationships that didn't satisfy her deepest need.

Noella's last romance had been over for more than three years when Tom Douten visited her classroom in January. She had dated sporadically in the meantime, guarding her emotions and words and never seeing the same man more than twice in a row. Never again would she say, "I love you," unless it was true.

By the time she met Tom, she had resigned herself to singleness. She would have loved decades of companionship, but not like the ones her parents had endured until her father's death six years before. He had been a professor of history at the University of Chicago, her mother a music teacher at a private high school. The Wrights had not been wealthy, but Noella was raised in comfort, if not security. To say her dad was less passionate and expressive toward her and her mother than the father figures she had read about or seen on the screen would have been kind. He was a brooding, distant, angry, troubled man. Still she felt fortunate. She hadn't been a college freshman long before she realized she was one of the few students whose parents were still married. Noella had always forced herself to look on the bright side.

Despite her father's temperament, their home had been one of surface refinement, of reverence toward education and filled with conversation that challenged the mind—and too often the spirit. At least William and Miriam Wright were can-do people. Noella assumed her outlook on life was a birthright.

In spite of her confidence, Noella had at first been impressed with Tom professionally and intimidated by him personally. Even when he finally agreed to address her students, she had not thought of him as a potential love interest, not even as a prospective date. She'd assumed he was married. He didn't carry himself like a man on the prowl. He was a functional dresser, pleasant-looking with honest, curious eyes.

She had worked hard to make sure the event went well. She E-mailed him nearly every day, making sure he was comfortable with her padding the audience with other journalism students as well as faculty. She asked if he would dedicate the last half to questions and answers. Would he come early for a refreshment reception? ("No, thank you.") He would, he said, arrange his schedule so he would not have to rush back to the city afterward.

He declined her request for a photograph for posters, so she copied and enlarged his column from the *Tribune* and used that.

He reminded her of his lack of formal education, and she assured him she was billing him as a working professional.

In those E-mails Noella got her first glimpse into the depth of his cynicism. He assumed her students were rich kids, materialists. He assumed the faculty consisted of lazy, tenured, unpublished theorists—except for her, of course. He assumed the university administration had its own agenda and took advantage of staff. He also assumed Northwestern suffered Ivy League envy.

Noella wanted to defend her students, her colleagues, her superiors, the university, and herself. But if he had come to such conclusions and formed such opinions without personal knowledge, she could not sway him. What had convinced this man that people were such takers? She hoped his talk wouldn't be one big downer. Perhaps big-time journalism eventually did this to a person.

TOM HAD TO admit, if only to himself, that the night was gorgeous. He pulled Noella close, fighting the urge to squeeze her so tightly they would melt together. He kissed her long and deeply, and he imagined he could breathe her whole being into his lungs. He felt her moist cheek against his as she whispered, "I love you so much." He knew she wanted more than another "me too," but expressing his love aloud had never been easy.

They looked up as a car rolled slowly over the packed snow toward the corner. The driver, an elderly man, gave them a thumbs-up, and they laughed.

"Your feet have to be cold by now," Noella said.

"I'm not cold anywhere right now," he said. They laughed again.

FOUR

Watching in the Night

TOM ALLOWED HIMSELF the luxury of a spacious two-
bedroom, two-bath unit in the Carl Sandburg apart-
ments on the Near North Side. The place was as large
as the tract house he had grown up in, and he was glad
his buddies and his family were over their initial awe.
When he had moved in three years before, he could
avoid for only so long having over his friends, his
brother and sister, and his parents. As he feared, from each
he got the standard la-di-da-aren't-we-the-millionaire-
now? Over time he had made the place uniquely his—
and, to his mother's surprise—pin neat.

Though the trip home from Round-the-Clock
was more tortuous than the trip out of the city, Tom

was distracted. He smiled at the thought of Noella's stunning necklace. How could a piece of jewelry retain such beauty for more than twenty years? It had to be more than a childhood trinket.

The snow kept coming. Fortunately the next day was Saturday, so Streets and Sanitation should make progress clearing the snow without heavy traffic.

At home Tom flipped on his answering machine. Just after noon his mother had called. "I hope you're not stuck out in this weather, Tommy. Your dad wants to know if you and Nola want to come watch rassling again Saturday night on TV. You don't need to call first. Just come on over."

The next call was from Walt Mathes, his boss. "T.D., it's me. I accessed the computer from home after getting word from Gary that you might not make your deadline. Course you always do, and you did, and I gotta tell ya, I'm glad I saw it. The mayor didn't come off too bad, and that's your second piece in a row without a tragedy in it. Listen, Monday we've got to talk about the Christmas editorial package. Anyway, good job and good night."

And Noella had called. "I miss you already sweetheart. I'd tell you how much I love kissing you, but who knows who might be there with you when you

hear this? Call me when you get in, no matter how late.
I won't sleep until I know you're safe."

Noella watched weather news on TV until Tom
called. She didn't intend to keep him up. He was the
one who kept talking.

"I can't quit thinking about that necklace," he said.
"It's beautiful."

"Next to my diamond, it's my favorite thing."

"It didn't come from your parents. They wouldn't
have gotten your birth date wrong."

"How many times do I have to tell you who I got
it from, Tom?"

"Well, you'd think Saint Nick would know your
birthday."

"That's always puzzled me too."

"It's a pretty nice present for a ten-year-old, especially if it didn't come from your parents. Who do you
think? Your grandparents? Your aunt?"

Noella responded with silence.

"Okay, stick with your story. But I'm gonna ask
your mother someday."

"You might not want to do that, Tom. She's not
real fond of it for some reason."

"Really? Wonder why."

"I'll never forget the looks my parents gave each other when I opened it. I said, 'Mom! Dad! Look what Santa sent me!' My mother looked at it very closely while my cousin and my aunt were opening presents. Mom smiled at first; then her smile faded, and she looked daggers at my father. I was confused. She said, 'How could you?' He asked to see it. She said, 'Don't pretend you don't know what it is.' He finally reached for it, and she stalled before handing it to him. He said it was small of her to cover her own mistake by accusing him of doing it."

"What did you make of all that?"

"I figured they didn't believe I got it from Santa. Each thought the other had given it to me."

"And nobody else would fess up?"

"I didn't ask. I knew who it was from."

"Oh, yeah. Santa. But surely you knew better by that age."

"Anyway, I'm glad you like it. I didn't take it off at first. I wore it in the shower. I wore it to bed. My parents accused me of being obsessed with it. One morning I woke up, and it was gone. I was hysterical."

"Where'd you find it?"

"Stuff doesn't just disappear. I made such a fuss

about it that my mother finally admitted she had taken it off in the night. She tried to tell me she was afraid it might catch on something and choke me. I demanded to know what she had done with it. Finally she said she would get it for me. I heard her digging through the wastebasket in her bedroom. She had actually thrown away my favorite possession! I was so mad I could hardly breathe, but I didn't tell her I knew what she'd done. I was just glad to have my necklace back.

"I didn't speak to her about it again. And I always tucked the pendant in, so she or Daddy couldn't see it. I was never as angry with my mother—even as a teenager—as I was that Christmas. Our relationship was strained for almost two years."

"She says you weren't a problem teenager," Tom said.

"I guess it was out of my system. She never did anything else so cruel or thoughtless. I got over it."

"I'd like to see the necklace again."

"Were you planning on seeing me between now and New Year's?"

"Only every possible moment."

"Then you'll see it all you want."

"Don't you wonder why the phrase isn't completed?"

"It's not necessary. Everybody knows 'Forever and a day.' "

Noella went to bed rehashing that strange Christmas of 1975, and all the old emotions resurfaced. Why couldn't she just enjoy the necklace and forget the past? Okay, so her parents weren't perfect. They'd tried. Noella sat up, angry that her memories and the emotions they evoked made it impossible to sleep.

She yanked her robe on and marched to the living room. Certain there would be nothing interesting on TV, she dug through her video collection and came across the tape of Tom's lecture to her class. It wouldn't put her to sleep, but it would put her mind on him rather than on her parents.

The first visage on the tape was her own, introducing "a nationally syndicated columnist who prefers being referred to as a reporter for the *Chicago Tribune.*"

His notebook, about two-thirds the width of a standard one, fitted in Tom's palm. "Thanks for having me," he said. "I'm more comfortable behind a keyboard than a lectern. It's a privilege to be referred to as a writer, and that's all I ever want to be called. This is new to me, and if I don't appear as nervous as I should, it's only because I finally realized I had something

I wanted to say to you, whether or not you want to hear it.

"It's only fair to admit that I am the least educated person in the room. I finished just a year and a half of college. Twelve years ago some of us could get away with that. It didn't make me antieducation. I have my problems with certain ways writing is taught, but these days the odds are stacked against anyone who wants to break into print without a diploma.

"With that out of the way, I want to tell you my own story as an example of how anyone from anywhere can realize a dream. I'll finish by revealing a simple approach to writing that guarantees an unending supply of material.

"I'm Chicago born and bred, grew up on the South Side. I went to Chicago Vocational High School, was a couple of spots from a starting position in three different varsity sports, am a Sox fan, still hang with two buddies from the neighborhood, and grew up in a home I didn't know was dysfunctional until TV talk shows told me.

"My father was a loudmouth, black and white, work-too-little, drink-too-much guy who was barely able to stay ahead of the wolf at the door. He's a recovering alcoholic, sober for several years. My mother is an enabler who finally became a doormat but whose kids still got the message that she cared for them in her own way. I have a brother two years younger, in prison for the third time for drug-related crimes. And I have a sister who still lives at home, works at a grocery store, and goes to beauty school.

"I'm the survivor, the one who escaped in spite of it all. From my family's perspective, any white-collar job is suspicious. In my mind, journalism saved my life. Being intrigued by and fascinated with words is a gift I can't take credit for. The only things I liked in school were English, writing classes, and sports. I quickly realized that writing was not a common gift, and I felt guilty that I could do something few others could. I worked on the school newspaper and covered sports and anything else I was assigned. I loved everything about journalism, from the clichéd who, what, when, where, and why to everything about putting a newspaper together.

"I caught on with a neighborhood paper, covering high school sports as a stringer. When I started going to a local community college, I took only journalism courses and badgered my way into a part-time job with the paper. I wrote everything from obituaries to the police log, but one day I found my niche, and the course of my career was set. Listen up and you won't have to discover it by accident like I did. I'm not worried about the competition because there's plenty of this out there for all of us."

Noella felt stupid smiling at Tom's image in the night. She hadn't even loved him when the video was taped. All she knew now colored how she listened to the man who had been a stranger not so long ago. She paused the tape and stepped into the kitchen to make herself a cup of warm milk.

Noella believed in fate. She had been destined to meet Tom and felt lucky to know him, to love him, and to have him love her. For more than twenty years she had clasped her most precious possession around her neck every December. That was how close she wanted to hold Tom every day for the rest of her life.

She tucked her feet under her in her recliner and started the tape again. "I was discovered," Tom told Noella's students, "an otherwise unprepossessing sports stringer who hung out in the offices of the *South Side Neighborhood Daily* and made a nuisance of himself. The editors told me they didn't have a full-time role for me, though they appreciated my help with the grunt work when I was finished with sports coverage. I tagged along to accident scenes with photographers because they wanted company and I had nothing else to do. Someone else covered the details, but I gravitated toward the victims. I came back with a slice of life, an impression, a quote or two, and the editor or the rewrite man folded them into the story. The reporter got the byline, and every once in a while I got a six-point credit at the end, 'Additional reportage by Thomas Douten.'

"Who noticed my stuff? Maybe the full-time reporters, I don't know. My guess is they saw me as a threat. But rewrite men and veteran editors appreciate someone with an eye for the germ of a story and the ability to put words together.

"They say big doors turn on small hinges, but the day one of those old-timers took me aside still seems like a huge hinge to me. John DiGiovanni smoked the smelliest cigars imaginable. He often worked the slot, but he also had a tiny office in the back where he invited cronies for a chat, especially after deadline. I wasn't yet twenty when he motioned that I should follow him back there. We never even sat down. He said, 'You know you're the best writer we've got, don't you?'

"I'd wished it, suspected it, but I never allowed myself to believe it. Until John said so.

"I said, 'So hire me.'

"He said, 'Can't do it. No money. Somebody gets sick, dies, moves, whatever, you're next. But if I were you, I wouldn't wait.'

"He called a buddy of his at the City News Bureau. Some of you work there already. Most of you will eventually. John told them to hire me and that they wouldn't be sorry. They did, and I had to be the only guy at the CNB who wasn't going to graduate even from community college. Whatever John had seen in my writing got squelched there. There was no room for flavor or flair. We were drones. We learned to find the story fast, get the facts, and get them filed. We worked all hours of the day or night. Those of us who loved it are still newspapermen. I don't know where the others are.

"I soon had a problem. I was stuck. I wanted to work for one of the big Chicago dailies, but both told me competition was so fierce that my chances were nil without a journalism degree.

"I went back to John DiGiovanni and told him, in all humility, that I thought I could write better than most of the J school interns I knew and about half of the people already writing for the *Sun-Times* or the *Tribune*.

"He said, 'Prove it.'

"I said, 'How?'

"He said, 'If I have to tell you, you're never going to make it.'

"I was getting paid so little I didn't mind adding a few hours to my day. What was the difference? On my own time I worked the same beats and the same streets. Before or after my shift at the CNB, I would find a story somewhere, bang it out, and deliver it. Anyone could have done it.

"I had trouble landing freelance news assignments. Guys told me, 'Try something for the tempo or life sections, features, stuff like that.'

"But that wasn't what I wanted to write. Nothing reached me like a story of life and death, grief, loss, pain, suffering. I didn't see that fitting the tempo section. Finally someone pointed me toward the cluttered desk of a man whose nameplate looked like an eye chart. His name was spelled J–a–n V–a–j–d–e. It was pronounced yon vidah. Jan had a thick Polish accent.

"Talk about a guy with printer's ink in his blood. He was known as the fastest, cleanest editor in the newsroom, and he loved everything about newspapering. Brash as I might have been chasing a story, I wasn't about to interrupt Jan Vajde and try to talk my way onto his staff.

"So I started dropping unsolicited manuscripts on his desk. The newsroom was so raucous that he didn't even notice me. He was loud and mercurial, and most reporters were afraid of him. When he wanted something, he shouted.

"Every night for several nights I dropped off a story, stood in a corner, and watched. I was thrilled when he finally got around to my copy. He read it, looked around, and read it again. Then he searched for it on-screen. Of course it wasn't there. He hollered, 'Who in the world is Thomas Douten?' and when no one answered, he studied the copy again, scratched a few edits on it, and put it in a stack at the corner of his desk.

"Finally I asked someone, 'How does a guy get next to Jan Vajde?'

" 'One surefire way,' I was told. 'Armpit pizzas.'

" 'I'm sorry?' I said.

" 'Thin-crust pizza, garlic, onion, and extra cheese. They smell like armpits. Deliver one at ten tonight. He'll love you forever.' With five stories languishing on Jan Vajde's desk, I showed up that night. He must have

smelled me coming. He looked up, delighted and ex-
pectant. I swear I almost said, 'Your armpit pizza.' What
I did say was 'Onion, garlic, and extra cheese.'

"Vajde actually blushed. He stood quickly, stuck his
stubby fingers deep in his pockets, and said, 'I'm terri-
bly embarrassed. I forgot I had even ordered. I'm gonna
have to borrow some cash from someone.'

"I told him it was paid for. He demanded, 'It is a
gift from whom then?' I told him Tom Douten. He
shouted, '*The* Tom Douten, the reluctant reporter?' He
pulled out three singles. 'Here's a tip at least. Introduce
me to Douten, and I'll scrounge up some more!'

"When I said, 'Speaking,' Vajde slammed both
palms on his desk and shouted, 'My new reporter is a
pizza delivery boy?'

"Vajde asked how old I was. I told him but also ran
down my experience, such as it was. I assured him I
would stay in college if that's what it took to work for
him. He told me to stay in college only if I wanted to
be his boss. I was among the last of the old breed. It
doesn't work that way anymore.

"I've had other offers, but obviously I never left the
Tribune. Never hope to. It's not perfect, and sometimes
it confirms my worst suspicions about corporations, but

a writer needs readers. For whatever its faults, the *Tribune* provides a platform wider than I deserve."

Noella fast-forwarded through a Q & A session and found Tom's conclusion.

"My challenge to you is to not run from hard stories, the everyday tragedies played out in the neighborhoods, the back alleys, the high-rises. There will always be plenty of reporters to cover everything else. There's room in the back of the news bus where I ride. You can't make a career on the dark side of the street just because there's unlimited story potential there, any more than a musician sings the blues just to tap into the market.

"If you're going to join me, bring your passion. The job will beat you up and sometimes make you despair, but with the right motive, abhorring shortcuts, giving every story all you have, you'll be able to look yourself in the mirror. You'll know you've used your gift to give voice to the speechless. If you keep honing your craft, your work just might expose a reader to the plight of someone he would never have occasion to meet.

"And I think that is a good and worthy thing."

Good and worthy, Noella thought as she slipped back into bed. That was Tom.

FIVE

Trouble in Paradise

It HAD NOT been love at first sight despite Noella's delicate beauty. Tom had been impressed with her tenacity. Intrigued even. But she was way too happy. How could anyone in her thirties at the end of the twentieth century—especially someone so bright and aware—have so much to smile about?

As he was on his way out of Medill, Noella said she hoped he would come back and do this again sometime. A sweetness about her began to work on him. She had confidence, and she was of course accomplished in her profession. He tried to reconcile that with her cloying optimism. Was he attracted to her? Who wouldn't be? Mostly he was curious.

She would never qualify as the subject of one of his

columns. Yet he did wonder what made her tick. "Are you free for lunch, by chance?"

They ate at a nearby bistro she recommended. "Your beautiful name," he said, "let me guess. A Christmas baby."

"The day after."

"Be glad you weren't born on Armistice Day."

A WITTY GUY *who loves to talk,* Noella thought. She found Tom funny, even if his humor was often, well, dark.

That night he had sent an E-mail: "A pessimist needs exposure to an optimist once in a while. Is the reverse also true? T. D."

She responded: "I can see where the pessimist would benefit; what's in it for the optimist?"

His reply: "Therapy?"

"Anything else?"

"Reality."

He suggested lunch at Tribune Tower. "Cool," she said. "I can pretend I belong there."

"You could work here," he said. "Your writing is facile."

"Serviceable, you mean?"

"You'll learn that *facile* is a genuine compliment from me."

"How will I learn that?"

"It might require time."

By the end of February they had seen each other half a dozen more times. The ice was finally broken one night when Tom seemed nervous after dinner and appeared to have to work up the courage to make a suggestion on the way to the car.

"How about dinner at my place next Friday?" he said.

She shot him a double take. "You cook?"

"Tube steaks are my specialty."

"Tube steaks?"

"You probably know them as hot dogs."

She laughed. "May I bring anything?"

He shook his head. "Just your buns."

"Um . . . How about I just bring the condiments?"

Tom shook his head again. "Never use 'em."

"An old line from *Rocky*. I'm impressed."

TOM FOUND HIMSELF nervous the following Friday. He finished his column early, a rarity, and spent the afternoon choosing just the right entrées for dinner. He didn't consider himself a gourmet, but he had learned to put together a nice meal of chicken breast and London broil. It required char-grilling both meats before baking the concoction over rice in the oven. He hoped his neighbors didn't notice him on the balcony, firing up the grill in the dead of winter. He hurried in and out, turning the meat, warming his hands over the charcoal.

For whom else would he go to such trouble? Noella was so radiant, so quick. And her students and colleagues lit up around her. Like a great pro athlete, a Michael Jordan, she made everyone around her better. *Especially me,* Tom thought.

By the time Noella showed up, Tom was happy with his work. He left catsup, mustard, and relish on the counter next to paper plates, just to see her reaction. He detected politeness and laughed. He could tell she was about to pretend to be thrilled with hot dogs.

"You want to help?" he asked.

"Sure."

"Help me put that stuff away. I can do better than that."

THE TINY TABLE near the window had been set with china, silver, and crystal. "I feel underdressed," Noella said.

"You look fabulous," he said. "And I'm ready to serve."

He pulled out a chair for her, and she sat and watched as he presented the food. "So, the caterers just left?" she said.

"Ouch!"

"Seriously, I'm impressed," she said.

"Ah, I cook like this for myself every day."

"And I'm the mayor. Hey, I smell charcoal. How'd you do this?"

He nodded toward the window.

"You didn't!"

"Look at the mess on the carpet."

Indeed, snow was melting just inside the sliding door. She shook her head. "You trying to make me feel special?"

"That shouldn't be hard."

Tom confessed the dessert was store-bought. "Can't go wrong with Eli's," he said.

"If you'd made the cheesecake, I'd be totally intimidated."

"But now you're only partly intimidated?"

She smiled.

"Hope you like Scrabble," he said.

"I'm no tournament player, but I love it. You play?"

"I play at it."

Noella insisted on helping clear and wash the dishes. "You'll take it easy on me, won't you? I don't know all the words the pros know."

"I plan to be a gentleman," he said.

"That's why I'm here."

"And as recreation director," he said, "I have one more surprise." He pulled a video from a Blockbuster bag.

"*Sleepless in Seattle!*" she said. "How did you know?"

"I just guessed."

"You guessed right," she said.

"You probably own it and have watched it dozens of times."

"Right again."

The Scrabble game deteriorated into hilarity as Tom drew ridiculous racks and made up words. "You've never heard of a ZIIL?" he said. "It's part of a ship or a bug or something."

He put the movie on. "I can cheat during the teary scenes," he said.

She sat next to him on the couch, the Scrabble board within reach on the coffee table. Tom leaned forward and dumped the rest of the tiles onto the board, fashioning a couple of words before sitting back again. Noella peeked.

"NOELLAS KOOL," she read.

She picked through the letters. "TOMS CRAZY," she wrote.

Tom added, "ABOUT NOELLA."

He draped an arm around her. She loved that he was the type that didn't talk during movies. And he didn't make fun of her when she cried. "I'm such a sucker for these things," she whispered, embarrassed. He reached for a box of tissues.

Noella didn't want the evening to end, but their relationship was still embryonic. As the credits rolled, she thanked him.

"Can we do this again sometime?" he said.

"Oh, maybe," she said. "At the very least I want you to come and cook for me if I have a guest."

"You couldn't afford me," he said.

TOM WALKED HER out. As they neared the door to the parking lot, he tugged at the fingers of one of her gloves and slipped it off. He drew her hand to his mouth. "Good night, Christmas Lady. Would you answer if I called you tomorrow?"

"On the first ring," she said, and they kissed.

LESS THAN A month later the calendar said it was spring, but an occasional flurry thumbed its nose at the groundhog.

Tom and Noella attended a Bulls game at the United Center, and from the national anthem to halftime, Noella could hardly hear herself think. Watching a Big Ten game at McGaw Hall was one thing. Pro basketball, especially Bulls style, was raucous. She found the game fast and exciting, and though Chicago had little competition that night, Noella was riveted.

Tom introduced her to Bart, a *Tribune* sportswriter, in the press box during halftime. "So, did you get here early enough to get the high-quality giveaway?" Bart asked.

Noella shook her head. "What is it?"

"A calculator from the Chicago Educational Association."

"Impressive," she said. "Wonder how they can afford that."

Bart said, "And what's in it for them? Are they hustling more students? They can't graduate the ones they've got."

Tom laughed. "The calculators are for figuring the salary of the one in a million dropouts who make the NBA."

"At least they're trying to do something positive," Noella said.

"Yeah," Tom said. "A two-dollar calculator more than makes up for the education I got."

"I learned more from my editors and colleagues than I ever did in class," Bart said.

"Course you didn't spend a whole lot of time in class!" Tom said.

"Probably the best thing that ever happened to me. Those who can, do. Those who can't, teach."

"The problem with *my* teachers," Tom said, "was that they could neither do nor teach!"

"Tell me about it."

Noella said, "I owe a lot to my teachers. Maybe I was just lucky."

"You sure were!" Tom said. "Course if I'd had a prof like you—"

"You'd have probably flunked out."

TOM'S SMILE FROZE. He was humiliated, Bart embarrassed.

The teams were warming up for the second half. "Back to the grindstone," Bart said. "Nice to meet you."

"Likewise," Noella said, but it was clear she didn't mean it. She was silent as they made their way back to their seats.

"What was that all about?" Tom asked as they sat.

"I should ask you," she said. "How was that supposed to make me feel?"

"We were kidding, Noella. You were rude."

"Bart was as boorish as you were. He makes fun of my profession, and you go right along."

Tom stared at her. "You're an outstanding teacher, Noella, but education as a whole—"

"If your friend was the writer you are, Tom, would he have devoted his whole life to sportswriting?"

"We're talking about education."

"You sure were, and I heard it loud and clear."

"It's true!" he said. "Present company excluded, journalism profs—"

"You can't exclude me, Tom."

"Fine! I'll include you. You'd have a lot more impact if you'd do what you teach."

"My writing is a hobby? Is that what you're saying?"

"I'm saying you should be a writer instead of a prof."

"You said yourself my writing was only facile."

"So, those who can, do, and those who can't—"

"You don't really think I can write."

"Forget it. I don't know what I think."

"That's clear."

Tom shook his head and looked away, pretending to be interested in the game.

"I knew this was going to happen," Noella said.

"What?" he said, turning back. He felt a heaviness in his chest. What was happening?

"Sue doesn't believe—"

"Sue?"

"She doesn't think we're a logical match."

"I should care what she thinks?"

"I'm not sure what you care about anymore," Noella said. They sat in silence for the rest of the third quarter. Noella could tell Tom was seething. Not until that moment had he reminded her of her father. She would not tolerate a future akin to her past, living with an accomplished man who smoldered. She wasn't about to give in just to make peace.

"Noella," Tom said, "I've seen you in the classroom. I know you're a great teacher."

"Tom, you have a real blind spot. Do you realize that not everyone enjoys your fearlessness? How many writers do you think believe they can write any story anytime?"

He shrugged. "Well," he said lamely, "you ought to be fearless, with the family you had, the support—"

"Sometimes I don't follow you at all. Don't make me tell you every detail of what appears an idyllic upbringing. You don't have a monopoly on pain."

Tom felt like an idiot. He couldn't find the words to apologize. He shook his head and tried to communicate with his eyes.

"I love you too," she said. "And you're not going to scare me off."

"I'm sorry," he said. "I was thoughtless."

"Temporarily not thinking maybe," she said. "But you won't be thoughtless till you're dead."

He leaned toward her, and she pecked him on the cheek. "One more crack about education," she whispered, "and I'll make you thoughtless."

SIX

A Pair of Queens

IN APRIL NOELLA had taken Tom home to meet her mother and grandmother. Miriam Wright was not yet sixty, but after her husband's death she had sold the family home and retired to a Glencoe condo with her late husband's mother.

Noella warned Tom of "two queens in the same hive."

The elder Mrs. Wright was in her mid-eighties, and when rising from a chair, she stood motionless for a moment to collect herself. Her hearing was going, but her mind seemed sharp. Noella's mother, Miriam, handsome and refined, was dressed elegantly. "I've never seen her otherwise," Noella confided.

Noella was impressed with how at ease Tom

seemed with the women. He engaged them in conversation and made them laugh. Over drinks in the music room after dinner, the elder Mrs. Wright propelled the conversation into another dimension. "So, Douten," she said, "are you going to marry this girl and put her mother's mind at ease?"

"Grandmother!"

"Oh, Rose!" Miriam said. "For Pete's sake!"

"Well," the old woman said, "it's what you want to know, isn't it?"

"I expect I will learn their intentions soon enough."

Rose leaned forward. " 'Soon enough' may not be soon enough when you're eighty-five."

Miriam scowled. "I wish you would show some class, Rose."

"Your people didn't have a corner on class, Miriam. At least nobody in our family—"

"All right!" Miriam shouted.

Noella recoiled. This was as loud as she had ever heard her mother. Miriam looked as if she were about to bolt, but Grandmother turned down the heat. She nodded toward Noella. "You'll love this one, Tom. She's a bit of a dreamer, but if you don't latch on to her, someday you'll wish you had."

"Rose," Miriam said, "you talk as if you'd raised this girl yourself."

Rose leveled her eyes at Miriam. "I wish I had. She's wonderful, but she's no child anymore, and she's still got her head in the clouds."

"The world could use more dreamers, Rose," Miriam said. "No offense, Mr. Douten, but I'd like to call it a night."

Noella went to help her grandmother rise and noticed her mother make a beeline for Tom. Later he told her that her mother had simply apologized for the old woman. "She said Rose was losing it. Frankly, I thought your grandmother held her own.

"Trust me, Noella," he said in the car. "I loved it. My dad told the truth only when he was hammered, and at the top of his lungs. Later he would cry and say he'd been lying about hating us or wanting us dead. Which do you think we believed?"

"Don't you owe it to a man to believe his remorse, especially when he's sober?"

Tom cocked his head at her. "You're an inveterate fixer, aren't you? Your mother and grandmother's arguing bothers you. My telling the truth about my father makes you uncomfortable."

"But look at you," she said. "You're not fixing *or*

facing it. Are you going to avoid your parents the rest of your life? If I were harboring bitterness or letting a problem fester, wouldn't you want me to get past it?"

"So it's my fault."

"Of course not. The home you grew up in didn't keep you from becoming a wonderful person, a gifted journalist."

"Then let me leave my past behind."

"I wish you would. I was embarrassed by my mother and grandmother's bickering in front of you, and all you could think of was how much better it was than your own home."

"It was!"

"When do you just accept your people and move on? I'm not asking you to pretend they're the Partridge Family. Just give them their due. Introduce me to them." She smiled. "We can make fun of them later."

Tom shot her a double take. "You'd scold me for that."

"Privately laughing at embarrassing relatives is different from pretending they don't exist."

By LATE SUMMER Noella had joined Tom at several Cubs and Sox games and regretted she'd dropped the one pastime she and her father had enjoyed together. She met Tom's high school buddies and their current wives (the second for one and the third for the other, and she was certain there would be more before they were through). She saw what he liked in the guys. They were straightforward, blunt, cynical. They were also loyal—at least to him, if not to their wives. They drank too much, but Tom never seemed to abuse alcohol.

At a fifth anniversary coffee celebrating Tom's column, Walt Mathes shook her hand and said, "So you're the one who's made him bearable."

Eve, a young editor, said, "I feel I know you already. Being in love has changed him, you know."

Noella refused to be drawn into comparing notes. It didn't surprise her that Tom might have been prickly to work with. She was grateful that others were starting to see in him what she saw.

She approached a huge man in a too-tight shirt and thrust out her hand. "You must be Rufus Young."

He roared. "And how did you know that?"

"Tom talks about you a lot."

"How did you know it was me? I look like a photographer?"

He had her trapped. "No. He just said you'd be the best-looking, most athletic guy in the room."

Rufus embraced her, laughing. "Anything else would have been slander."

Noella fell into easy, serious conversation with Rufus. "Tom thinks the world of your work, and so do I."

Rufus leaned close. "You know how much that rascal loves you, don't you?"

"I'm getting the picture."

Rufus laughed. "Great line to use with a photographer. I'm just saying, I can see it written all over him. He never had to win me over because I knew he had the goods as soon as I started reading his stuff. He writes the way I want to shoot. We hit it off because neither of us has much patience with bull. Me because I'm older 'n God, him because I don't know why. Not too many people cared for him around here. He wasn't too big for his breeches or anything. He just stayed to himself, and that made people nervous. A year ago he would have skipped his own party or convinced the brass not to do it."

"He was reluctant about this," Noella said.

"He's proud of you. He has reason to be."

"Whatever people like about him has been there all along."

"He's in love. If that doesn't thaw somebody's parts, nothing will."

"I've changed too," she said.

That night after the party Tom retrieved something from the glove box before walking Noella to her door. He kissed her and handed her a single rose.

"So I'm more than just someone to show off?" she said.

He nodded.

"Then say so."

"You know."

"I want to hear it."

"I love ya."

"Who's 'ya'? For a man of letters, you're a man of few words."

"I do, you know," he said.

"Slow down. You can't get to 'I do' without going through 'I love you.'"

"I know."

"You *know* I love you, Tom, because I tell you."

TOM HAD FINALLY taken Noella to meet his parents in August. As he drove to the South Side, he said, "I have to explain a few things before we get there."

"Don't feel obligated."

"I'm not sure you understand how far apart our cultures are."

Noella had been sitting close, her hand on his thigh. She pulled away. "Tom, don't overdramatize this. It's not some tragic play: Rich girl falls for poor boy. I've always looked for intelligence and ambition in a man. I have no complaints."

"But what if I wanted you to live in a neighborhood like the one I grew up in?"

"I'd live anywhere with you."

"You're too good to be true."

"Spare me."

"I just want to prepare you for our house."

"I know. It's small, it looks like the others on the street, no garage. One bath, small rooms. I get it, Tom. Your parents aren't wealthy. It's okay."

"Most people my parents' age at least have equity. They've been in that house since before I was born, but every time it increased in value, they refinanced."

"Wouldn't they be embarrassed if they knew I knew that?"

"There you go again, fixing everything. Embarrassment is not an issue with them."

"If I said that about your family, you'd call me elitist."

"Just let me vent," he said.

"Nice yard," she said as he pulled in behind his mother's car.

"Mom must have cut it. Her idea of putting on airs."

His mother met them at the door. "Charles!" she called out. "She's here!"

"That time already?" Mr. Douten said, turning off the TV. He shook Noella's hand and hurried away.

"I forgot to warn you about the smell," Tom said.

"I've been around smokers."

The Doutens returned, he tucking in a white shirt. "I'm starved, Dot," he said.

Tom cringed as they crowded around the kitchen table.

After a meat and potatoes dinner, Mrs. Douten served four huge helpings of strawberry shortcake, each in a plastic cereal bowl.

"You like rasslin', Noella," she said quietly.

"Who doesn't?" her husband said.

"Professional wrestling? I don't guess I've ever really watched a whole, um, fight."

"You haven't?" Mr. Douten said. "You're in for a treat. Huge championship tonight."

"Tom and I have been enjoying lots of pro sports."

Tom shook his head. "I'd hardly call—"

Noella put a hand on his arm. "We can't stay late, but I'd love to watch with you."

"Tonight they rassle for the international title," Mrs. Douten said.

It was clear Tom's parents bought the whole package. Mrs. Douten, when her husband wasn't shushing her, explained how important this match was to the challenger. "He's suing his former manager for a billion dollars," she said from her spot on the floor, "and there's a good chance he'll get it."

It was all Noella could do to keep from laughing. Mrs. Douten squeezed in next to her. With Tom on one side emitting barely audible groans and his mother on the other explaining everything, Noella was having the time of her life.

"He not only gypped him out of his title," Dorothy Douten said, "but said awful things about his wife."

"So this is personal," Noella said.

"It's a grudge match. It really is."

"I should think he'd care more about his wife than about the money."

"Probably. But a billion . . ."

By the end of the evening the Doutens were giddy.

Their man had won. "That's an omen," Mrs. Douten said. "I bet he wins the billion too."

"Wouldn't that be perfect?" Noella said. Tom was pulling her out the door.

Mrs. Douten winked at Noella. "It'll all turn out the way it's supposed to."

SEVEN

Every Tomorrow

TOM AND NOELLA had been seeing each other at least every other day for weeks. Noella was in love and believed Tom was. He showed it in different ways, though ironically, words still seemed to fail him. Their times together seemed to take on a more formal air. Noella felt as if she were being courted the old-fashioned way.

Friday-night dinners at swanky places highlighted the last three weeks of September. On his other deadline nights they still met late at the Round-the-Clock, but a visit to the Mrs. Wrights in Glencoe also popped up.

"Your mother called me," Tom told her one day.

"You're kidding."

"Asked me to join her and her mother-in-law for

dinner Tuesday evening. Said I should feel free to bring a guest."

"What would keep you?"

"If I can't find a date."

"Do I have a shot?" she said.

"The decision of the judges will be final."

The elder Wrights were charming that night. Grandmother insisted on a private chat with Tom. Noella's mother set her jaw and rolled her eyes at Noella. "Would you just marry this guy so Rose gets the message that she doesn't have a chance?"

In the car later Noella said, "What is Grandma's obsession with you?"

"No mystery," Tom said. "We're both single."

"Yeah, but I've got dibs."

"All's fair . . ."

ON THE LAST Friday of September, Noella stayed late in her office working on a piece for *Chicago* magazine. She and Sue were going out for Chinese at six; then Noella planned to work at home until it was time to meet Tom at Round-the-Clock.

At five-thirty he called. "I finished early," he said. "How about meeting in half an hour?"

"Where?"

"The usual. We've never actually had dinner there."

"I can't say I've missed that, but sure—oh, no, Tom! I've got dinner with Sue. I'm sorry. See you later? Regular time?"

"No, you don't," Sue said from the doorway. "I tried to call you, but your line was busy. I need to beg off. I'm coming down with something."

"Are you all right?"

"Just a bug. I'll be fine."

It wasn't like Tom to beat his deadline, let alone by several hours. Noella couldn't remember his having beaten her to Round-the-Clock either. But when she arrived, straight from the office in sweater and slacks, he was in their booth with his coffee—and wearing a suit and tie.

"I didn't know you owned a suit," she said, leaning in to kiss him.

"It's new. I thought maybe they had a dress code at this time of the day."

Noella slid into the booth. "We can go someplace nice. I'm a little underdressed, but we might still be able to get in somewhere."

"Not on a Friday night," he said. "This will be fine.

I just wanted you to see my suit. Don't get used to it. With only one, I have to pick my spots."

"What's the occasion?"

"Celebrating finishing early for once."

"Early enough to have a suit fitted and still beat me here?"

"I must have known I was going to have a good day."

Noella studied him. When was the last time he had bought himself anything but a box seat ticket or something for his computer?

"And we're celebrating finishing your column ahead of schedule? I guess that won't happen too often."

"Touché."

After dinner Tom waved at Rita. Noella laughed when she delivered two orders of strawberry shortcake in cereal bowls, piled high with whipped cream. "Perfect," she said. "Could you have Rita switch the TV to pro wrestling?"

Tom's spoon arrived buried so deep in the whipped cream that when he took a bite, the cream touched his nose. Noella dabbed it with her napkin. The same thing happened on the next bite. "Sweetheart, just wipe that off your spoon."

"No way," he said. "I'm going to eat every last bit."

"Then lick it off."

"Sounds uncouth."

"In *this* restaurant? You could use your sleeve."

Noella sighed when he smeared his nose with the whipped cream yet again.

"What?" he said. "You want to switch spoons?"

"Yes, let's. I'm not afraid to lick it off."

"Right here in the Round-the-Clock?" he said.

Noella licked the whipped cream off, but when she reached the point where the handle widened into the spoon blade, she felt something loose with her tongue. A diamond ring had been slipped over the end. Tears came before she could form a response. She removed the sticky ring from the spoon and stared as Tom gently took it, swished it in the water glass, dried it on a napkin, and slid out of the booth onto his knee next to her.

It all hit her at once. His talks with her mother and grandmother. The invitation to her mother's. Dinner instead of late-night coffee. Sue's bug. Tom's suit. Obviously, Rita had been involved. In Noella's peripheral vision, people whispered, nudged, pointed. Soon the whole place fell silent, waiting.

Tom held the ring up to the light. "Isn't it beautiful?"

"Yes."

"I need another yes, Noella. You've become my whole life. Every yesterday before you pointed to today. I'm asking for your tomorrows."

Noella fought to make herself heard. "All I have is yours, Tom. Including every tomorrow."

He slipped the ring on her finger. An old man two tables away called out, "Was that a yes?"

"Yes!" Noella said. And the restaurant erupted in applause.

EIGHT

Humbug

By Monday, November 30, the snowstorm had passed through and temperatures rose. No one figured the snow would be totally gone before spring because Chicago was unlikely to warm up before March. But Streets & San transferred mountains of salt to trucks that spread it over every inch of the area's expressways, streets, and roads. Removing stranded cars was tedious, but the city was soon moving again, and schools were open.

Tom soon had to get started on his annual Christmas piece. It ran on the front page, usually a couple of days before Christmas, and was at least twice as long as his normal column. Tom was embarrassed by the response it engendered, but it had become a tradition.

Newspaper people believed that any response was better than no response and that those who threatened to cancel their subscriptions rarely did.

Tom usually wrote a more involved story similar to his column. Someone had suffered an unspeakable loss, and Tom asked what Christmas and all that went with it would do for that person. Letters poured in, readers telling how the spirit of Christmas had healed sick children, brought families together, brought gifts to orphans at the last moment. Urban legends, Tom decided. And he often said so.

Some readers asked how the *Tribune* could allow this annual desecration of a beautiful holiday. The paper never defended itself. It allowed readers to vent and Tom to keep up the tradition. It didn't seem to hurt the popularity of his regular column. Research showed he had more readers than most columnists in the country.

LATE THAT MONDAY morning three reporters, another columnist (Gary Noyer), and a page editor joined Tom in Walt Mathes's office. Walt scribbled on a flip chart everyone's ideas for the Christmas editorial package, which would begin running mid-month.

There would be something on the number of Santa

suits rented in the metropolitan area, an update on the Toys for Tots charity the *Tribune* supported, a short-short contest for young people, a recurring My Favorite Christmas piece, and something on households that celebrated both Christmas and Hanukkah.

Tom nodded when Walt asked, "The usual?"

Gary Noyer said, "What'll the wet blanket consist of this year, Douten?"

"I'm noodling two things. One is the lies parents tell their children at Christmas."

"Charming."

"The other is about a guy who doesn't want one rational piece in the paper about Christmas but would rather we leave our brains under the tree until New Year's."

"Me?"

"Could I get with you for an interview?"

"Shut up, Douten."

"Gentlemen, please," Mathes said.

NOELLA HAD LUNCH that day with Sue Beaker to ask her an important question. But Sue had to debrief first. "If Bernard were only a little more energetic . . ."

"What did you expect?" Noella asked. "You

said you wanted to slow down when you married him."

"He's in his sixties, I'm in my forties—though I don't look it, do I? Please lie to me."

"You don't look like you're in your forties at all," Noella said.

"Bless you."

"I would have guessed fifties."

"Witch."

"Now there's a nickname for me," Noella said.

"You never had this mean streak before you met Ebenezer."

"You know I was teasing. You're in great shape, you're gorgeous, and you don't look a day over thirty-five."

"But I do look mid-thirties, don't I? There's no getting away with the 'same age as Noella' line, is there?"

"Please! So your husband is older? You wanted security."

"But that's so sexist. Security is one thing, but when I want to go dancing, Bernie wants to sit on the porch and read the paper."

"In this weather?"

"You're such a literalist."

If she only knew, Noella thought.

Noella told Sue of her hope to be married by the end of February.

"I love it!" Sue said. "And I'll do anything you want, punch bowl, guest book, you name it."

"I was hoping matron of honor."

Sue put her hand on her chest, and her eyes filled. "I've never stood up for anyone before. Are you serious?"

"It doesn't take experience."

"But you have lots of friends your own age."

"Think of it as a way to make people think you *are* my age."

"I cherish our friendship, but I never dreamed—"

"You're like a sister, Sue."

"A big sister."

"Stop it."

"But I've said awful things about Tom."

"That'll have to stop," Noella said.

"Yeah. I'll probably have to start liking him and everything."

"That should be easy."

"If you love him," Sue said, "I can learn to like him."

"You make it sound like a chore."

Sue put a hand on Noella's arm. "I want to be sure you're using your head and not just following your heart."

As they stood at the cash register, Noella said, "Support my decision, because I'm not looking back."

"You would if you had second thoughts, though, right? I mean, a broken engagement is only embarrassing. A failed marriage is a disaster."

"I don't foresee either. Nothing has ever seemed so right."

"Forgive me," Sue said as they drove back to Medill. "Can I still be in the wedding?"

"Just give me the benefit of the doubt. I've spent the better part of this year with Tom. We belong with each other. I've never been surer of anything in my life."

"Then I'll trust you. But I worry."

"Quit worrying. I'm a grown woman. I wasn't desperate for a man. I found a soul mate, and I love all the best things about him."

"And the rest?"

"The rest is no worse than me at my worst."

"You at your worst is better than most at their best."

"That's something Tom would say."

"Then I would like him."

"You'll love him. You just need to get to know him."

"You think he'd like to double-date with another gorgeous J school prof . . . and her father?"

THAT NIGHT RITA brought Tom's coffee and Noella sipped hot chocolate.

"Do you ever take off that necklace?" Tom said.

"Sure. Why?"

"I'm asking whether I can see it."

She took it off and held it out to him so lovingly that Tom knew he had been entrusted with her most precious possession. He took it in both hands and turned it in his fingers. "It still looks new. Have you had it cleaned?"

"I wipe it with tissue now and then, that's all."

"It gleams like platinum, but surely that's just platinum color, don't you think?"

"I've never thought about it."

Tom examined it in the light. There should be some wear in the surface after more than twenty years. Even up close it appeared solid. Solid what, he didn't know. Platinum would have been no small gift. He let the pendant rest right side up in his palm, the chain draped through his fingers. "Spectacular," he said. The chain was made of the same material as the pendant. "I wouldn't know gold from fake, but for this to still be so beautiful after so long—"

"The necklace or the fiancée?"

Tom dangled the pendant before his eyes and peeked at Noella through the tree-shaped cutout. "You do it justice."

"Are you planning to keep it?" she asked.

"I'll keep you," he said. "And then I'll always have it." She leaned forward, and he reached to clasp it at the back of her neck. Her eyes were inches from his. He fastened the necklace but left his hands there. "I could look at you forever."

Tom settled back and realized Rita was standing there. "I was going to warm up your coffee," she said, "but you probably did it yourself."

A few minutes later Noella said, "Can we talk about the wedding?"

"I'll show up."

"Tom, that's so Neanderthal. I want this to be really ours, not just mine."

"Can I ask for black crepe paper and gloomy music?"

"You're not excited about it?"

"I just want to be sure my personality is represented."

"You can't fool me with that anymore. You're a softy, and everyone will be on to you before long. We've got to think about colors, order of service, number of attendants and bridesmaids—"

"You'd better limit it to three. Rufus will be best man if I can find him a big enough tux. You met the other two, and they're going to have to double as ushers. That's the extent of my friends."

"Not Walt?"

"Nah."

"That Gary guy?"

"No!"

"Your dad or your brother, if he's out by then?"

"Get serious."

"Tom, think about that. They'd be thrilled. And down the road you'll wish you had included them. Family is forever."

"Don't remind me. Tim will probably still be in prison."

"I want you to enjoy the process."

"Just tell me how to get the tux on and the dress off."

"Thomas."

Tom told Noella of an interview he'd conducted that afternoon not far from his own childhood home. "Rufus put me on to him. Single father, raising three kids. Not my kind of a story, but it'd be perfect for the magazine, except for some Santa stuff. You ought to do it."

"What Santa stuff?"

"He tells his kids the truth. They enjoy Santa as a myth, but he makes it clear Santa isn't real, like Mother Goose."

"Why spoil it for them?"

"His kids didn't seem any the worse for wear."

"But how would you know?" she said.

"At least they won't have to find out later."

"Find out what?"

"About Santa."

"Give me the guy's address," she said, sighing.

"It was just a suggestion," Tom said, wondering what he had done to irritate her. He reached for her across the table, but she hesitated. He sat back. "I'm not real big on Christmas," he said, "as you've probably noticed from my columns."

"Your annual bah-humbug? You do it on purpose.

What would the *Tribune* do without all those letters condemning you?"

"I don't do it for the response. I really believe the Christmas thing is ridiculous. It's the saddest time of year for a lot of people. They believe their problems will be solved, their relationships mended. It's become the holiday that doesn't deliver."

Tom wished he hadn't gotten into it. Whatever had set her off, this diatribe wasn't helping. Her look had gone from angry to sad.

"I'm not talking about you, sweetheart," he said. "The joy you take in the beauty, the snow, the Santa thing, that all makes you who you are."

"One Christmas with me, Tom, and you'll look forward to the rest of them we spend together."

"But you're marrying the bah-humbug guy."

"That tune is old. How many ways can you say Christmas isn't as great as most people think?"

"That's just it, hon. Kids in the ghetto actually believe Santa is going to bring them something to make their lives all right. Mama can't afford it, so she says maybe Santa will bring it. Problem is, Mama knows better."

"Those parents don't really believe what they're saying," Noella said.

"Of course they don't, but the story gets the kids through another cold month. Whoopee. Merry Christmas."

"If those parents really believed, the outcome would be different."

"What's to believe?"

Noella did not answer. Tom had lost her gaze. And more. It was as if he had pulled her plug.

NINE

Too Close for Comfort

Tom was not sleeping well. Ever since his disparaging of Christmas, he'd felt a distance between Noella and him. They continued seeing each other almost every day and even discussed wedding plans, yet something had changed. There was less eye contact, less of what Tom could only describe as a soul connection. Had it been unrealistic to hope their passion would always be at fever pitch? The more he sought to reproduce the magic, the more elusive it became.

When he probed, Noella didn't budge. She said she was fine. She said she loved him, but said it not so frequently. She returned his embrace and his kisses and said she looked forward to their life together. What more did he want? He didn't know.

By Friday, December 4, Tom wondered about his sanity. He looked for a logical explanation, something simple. If he could get a handle on it, he could fix it. Noella told him he was imagining things, but he knew better. You learn a person after loving them nearly a year, he told himself, and something was out of whack.

Tom's frustration affected his work. He had no energy. He worked out less frequently and then not at all. He answered memos with a word or two. He was short-tempered with colleagues. "Your girl mad at you or something?" Gary Noyer suggested.

"Drop dead," Tom said.

"That's the Douten I know," Noyer said.

Tom wanted to kill him. What was happening?

He fashioned a few serviceable columns, but his annual Christmas piece was going nowhere. He and Noella were simply going to have to have it out.

NOELLA DIDN'T LIKE Tom's tone when he called late that morning. He wanted to get together earlier again.

"You going to wear a suit? Bring another ring?"

"No, and I don't want to meet at Round-the-Clock either. I just want to talk."

"Anything serious?"

"I hope not."

"This is your idea, Tom. You ought to know."

"How about right there on campus?"

"I'll be here. When are you going to write your column?"

"I know my schedule, Noella."

"Will you make your deadline?" He didn't respond. "I guess that's not my worry."

"My sentiments exactly."

"Tom, is something wrong? Have I—"

"Isn't that what I've been asking you for the past week?"

Noella knew exactly what was wrong. She was scared she would never penetrate Tom's anti-Christmas bias. Maybe it was more important to her than it should have been, but she would never say that aloud. That much vulnerability could cost her the love of her life. While she wasn't ready to tell him the truth, clearly she couldn't hide the distance between them. She would have to take some blame, do better at covering, somehow allay his suspicions. The depth of her passion for the season was the only thing between them.

THE CLOSER TOM got to Evanston, the more manic he felt. When he pulled in, Noella waved from her office and signaled that he should wait there. When she came down, she carried a blanket. They did not embrace. He couldn't shake his angry expression. She looked wary, and he couldn't blame her. He hated having to be so direct but was desperate to clear the air.

Should he demand to know what had caused the distance between them? Should he blame her for his loss of sleep, his irritability? Should he tell her things had to change? Not knowing what to say was worse than having planned the wrong thing.

Noella led him to a bench beside a little-used walkway. She brushed snow off it, spread the blanket to insulate their seats from the cold, and sat. How could she be so loving, so take-charge, after he had attacked her on the phone? She put an arm around him. With her face close to his, she said, "Talk."

"I don't feel close to you," he said.

"Too bad. You're my fiancé, and I love you. Whatever it is, get it on the table. You can't scare me off, even if you want to."

If HE *HAD* wanted to turn her away, Noella could have done nothing about it. The distance he had detected was not intended to push him away. She was not ready to risk her future with him by giving it voice.

Tom came right at her. "You aren't the same. You've pulled away, and I want to know what's up. Did I do or say something?"

"It wasn't you, Tom. It was me."

"That's such a cliché! What was happening with you?"

"I hardly know myself," she said. "But it should make you feel better to know that I know what's bothering you. It was me, and I will change. You're the center of my life, and it's going to show from now on."

Tom WAS AT a loss. If he had dreamed of an explanation, he could not have come up with such a satisfying answer. Was that it then? Her fault? No big deal? He gets mad, points it out, she sees it, caves, and everything's back to normal?

Then why had he had to endure such grief? "I need some sleep," he said, shoulders drooping.

"I need a kiss," she said, and he responded hungrily. He felt her tears on his face and had to fight his own. "Now go do your column on deadline," she said. "Meet me later, usual time, usual place."

"I'm sorry if something I said made you—"

"I told you, Tom, it was my fault."

"But still, I—"

She covered his mouth with hers. "Write a killer column," she said finally.

Tom returned to Tribune Tower energized as if he had slept twelve hours but still wondering what was going on.

TEN

Of Trust and Truth

THAT AFTERNOON NOELLA could not concentrate. Her discussion with four grad students was a disaster. Normally she steered the conversation, pushing the two men and two women beneath the surface of local news coverage in several major cities. But her attention drifted. When she should have wrestled an argument back into a discussion or rescued an awkward silence with an apt question, her mind was elsewhere.

"I apologize," she said finally. "Let's try this again next week."

Noella returned to her office, grateful no one else was around. She felt as guilty about what she had kept from Tom as if she had told him an outright lie. A grown woman and she hadn't learned the art of deception.

Noella had trained herself to put the shoe on the other foot. Would she want Tom to mislead her, even for her own good? But her deceit wasn't for Tom's good. It was to protect her. In truth she was more than an optimist. More than a Pollyanna. She didn't just love Christmas and everything that went with it. There was something she hadn't told him. She felt like a liar.

Noella wanted to look forward to seeing Tom, but the idea of facing him without his knowing everything made her dread their meeting that night. She loved the devotion in his eyes. Here was a man with a brain, a cause, a passion, and she had his full attention. But he was also insightful. She had soothed him with her performance several hours before, but there would be no hiding from the searchlight of a man in love. Her cursed conscience was sure to imprint itself on her face or in her body language. And try as she might to act the way she felt—hopelessly in love—the very object of that love would ferret out the distance again. He would be frustrated. Maybe angry. And he would have a right to be.

They had learned the deep things about each other. They had discussed previous relationships, what had been right, what had gone wrong, what they had learned. If they agreed on anything, it was an absolute commitment to honesty. He had made it clear that he would ask her to marry him only if she shared his bedrock commitment to mutual trust. He had asked and she had answered, and she believed they were committed to each other for life. In her mind their promises were set in stone.

Tom knew everything about her except one thing. Had it been an infidelity, she would have worried more about the offense than the hiding of it. But it was merely an anachronism, something he might accept in a child but not in a woman. And because of the kind of a man he was, she feared it would cost her his respect.

Noella sat at her desk as the sun went down and the room grew dark. She hadn't moved since she returned from class. A heaviness in her chest developed into a sob she swallowed away until she couldn't stop the tears. Shoulders slumped, head down, hands in her lap, she sat weeping. Should she grow up, cast aside her craziness? Would she hold to a childish faith at the expense of true love? Not rationally. But she couldn't just decide to quit believing something she desperately needed to believe.

Noella jumped at a young female voice. "Excuse me, Dr. Wright. Are you okay?"

Noella nodded. "Just resting a moment," she said, her voice thick. She cleared her throat. "I'm fine, really. Thank you."

The student studied her and left.

Noella moved, dreamlike, to her coat tree. Before she pulled on a long white coat, she peeked at her Christmas pendant, ran her thumb over the cutout, and tucked the necklace inside her sweater. She could prolong the inevitable for only so long. She drove the streets of Evanston. She saw a snow-covered path they had walked, a bench they had sat on, a park where they had strolled in the snow and where they had kissed for hours. She drove past Round-the-Clock and then toward the outer drive. Festive decorations along the route wounded her.

Noella would maintain the charade no longer. Heading south toward the city now, she called Tom on her cell phone.

"Hey, babe!" he responded. "You inspired me today! I almost wrote that single father piece myself. But it's still yours if you want it. I'm almost done with my column. I'll read it to you later."

"If you want to."

He hesitated. "What's up?"

"You want to meet downtown somewhere, hon? You always come this way."

"Where do you want to go?"

"I'm on the Drive. How about the Chop House?"

"Think they'll let us just sit and talk?"

"I'll call, and I'll wait for you on Michigan."

TOM DIDN'T WANT to jump to conclusions. Noella had sounded all right, but not as warm as she'd been that afternoon. He finished his column and hurried to the elevator. He jogged across Michigan Avenue and got into her car. She leaned over and held him fiercely. She had been crying. "Whatever's wrong," he said, "I hope you're still gonna marry me."

"If you'll have me," she said, pulling into traffic.

She turned right on Wacker and then onto Orleans and parked at the Merchandise Mart. They walked to the Chop House. The maître d' was expecting them. "Quiet booth in the back, just beverages."

They sat, and Tom expected Noella to jump in with what was on her mind. She didn't. "I love you so much, Tom."

"But—?"

"But I disagree with you about Christmas."

He smiled. "No way! You don't hate Christmas as much as I do?"

"Don't tease me. We're diametrically opposed on this."

He sat thinking. "It has to be a serious issue?"

"Maybe."

"It'll threaten our future if I keep writing bah-humbug pieces?"

"I know what I'm getting with you," she said. "You're the one who's been deceived. You don't realize where I am."

"This is pathological? You're so into Christmas that, what, you have a secret identity?"

"This isn't easy, Tom. Don't make light of it."

Tom wished she would just come out with it. The waiter brought their coffee and hot chocolate. Noella ignored hers.

"You're being indirect, hon," he said. He reached to caress her cheek, but she didn't lean toward his touch. He slipped a finger into her necklace and gently pulled until the pendant dropped into sight. "Think anything you like about Christmas, Noella. You were born at Christmas for Christmas. It goes with your personality."

NOELLA WANTED TO scream. He was such a great investigative journalist, why couldn't he figure it out for himself? He had missed all the signals. She would have to force the issue.

"Still wondering where I got the necklace?"

"Had to be your grandmother. For it to hold up so beautifully over the—"

"Tom. My grandmother would know my birthday."

"Your aunt then? Maybe she just got the date wrong."

"My aunt was a widow who could barely afford to get to our house for Christmas."

"We've ruled out your parents."

She nodded. "I got it from Santa."

"And you know that because . . ."

"It said so on the package."

"There you have it. If he wrote it on the box, well—"

"You're making light again."

"You don't want me to make light of Santa?"

"Of course I don't."

"Or of the fact that he brought your necklace?"

"Definitely don't make light of that."

TOM SQUINTED. She was serious. "Why?" he asked quietly.

Noella would not return his gaze. "You wouldn't like it if someone made fun of something that important to you."

"I'm not making fun of Christmas, hon! Not even of Christmas spirit, the joy of giving, all that."

"Santa is part of that."

"You talk about him like he's a person."

"He *is* a person."

"I mean, a real person."

"That's what I mean."

Tom sat back. There was a wall again, and he sensed he had created it. "Okay," he said. "Any other Christmas items or people or ideas I should revere?"

"No."

"I just want to get the lay of the land," he said. "Tell me where the mines are. You're worth it."

She looked at him. He decided that was progress. "What if I told you I still believed in Santa Claus?" she said.

"You've made that clear."

"But I mean, really."

"I'm sorry?"

"I literally, really, actually—I don't know how else to put it, Tom—believe in Santa Claus. Am I still worth it?"

There had to be an answer. "Hypothetically, right?"

"You're dodging," she said.

"Is this going to be on the final?"

Noella leaned forward until she was inches from his face. "Tom, this is the final."

"But surely you're being—"

"Hypothetical? How does hypothetical fit with literally, really, actually?"

Tom's pulse surged. Did she want to know if he would accept anything she said? It was a no-win. He was a wuss if he supported every fool thing, yet he had already suffered for disparaging Christmas.

He moved his lips so she could see he was rehearsing. "Okay, what would I say if she said she still believes in Santa Claus and she actually means it? Would she still be worth it? Sure. Loony, but worth it. Better not say that. Would I still love her and want to marry her? Sure. Wait. If she really, really means it?"

Tom placed his palms on the table. "I need more clues. Obviously this is rhetorical."

She put her hands over his, and he felt her tremble.

"Okay, Tom, here it is. Not hypothetical. Not theoretical. Not rhetorical, all right? I *know* Santa came to my house when I was ten, and I *know* he gave me my necklace!"

Tom forced a smile. Her eyes were locked on his.

"You deserve to know everything about me," she continued, "and that's it. I'm not going to lie. I'm thirty-two years old, a Ph.D., a fully functioning adult. And I believe in Santa Claus. I know I'm in a very small minority, but there it is."

Tom sat back. "What are you, serious?"

Noella appeared to disintegrate. She slid out of the booth, and he quickly reached for a ten. "Noella! Wait!" By the time he slapped the bill on the table and grabbed his coat, she was out the door. "Noella!"

He caught her as she strode toward the Mart parking lot. "I'm sorry, hon. I put my foot in it here somehow, and I haven't even figured out how." She wouldn't look at him. "I'm not going to chase you like a puppy," he said. "I'm playing without a rule book here. I have no idea what point you're trying to make." She kept walking. "Ah," he said, "forget it!"

ELEVEN

Torn Apart

NOELLA DROVE TO her apartment, marched in, and slammed the door. Standing in the middle of the room with her hands in her coat pockets, she thought, *I shouldn't have left. We're stalemated.*

She was buzzed from the foyer. "It's me."

She didn't respond.

"Buzz me in, Noella. Please."

"Stay there," she said. "I'm coming down."

Noella dreaded facing him. But he had come after her, she had to give him that. And she didn't want to face another day without everything on the table.

She would step off the elevator directly into his view. Would he be furious? Noella wasn't mad anymore. Just desperate. She felt sheepish as she stepped out, then at a loss when Tom merely looked lovingly at her. She walked through the security door and stopped at the top of the steps. "Come here," he said, opening his arms. Noella descended slowly. "I'm sorry," he said, gathering her in.

"It's not your fault, Tom."

"You don't ever have to walk away from me. You're obviously trying to tell me something. Now talk to me."

"I have nothing more to say, Tom. I already told you. Take it seriously. I won't fault you for any reaction."

He looked away. "I'm sorry. I don't follow. I'm supposed to find some meaning in the Santa thing?"

"There's no hidden meaning."

He raised his hands and let them drop. "Please, Noella. I'm a straightforward, black-and-white guy. I'm not trying to be unkind, but whatever you're trying to say, spell it out."

Noella shook her head. "This is the last time. Listen to me, hear me. I believe in Santa Claus. I believe he's real. I wrote him a note when I was ten, and I asked him somehow to make it a good Christmas for my cousin, whose dad, an uncle I never saw, had been dead for years. She and my aunt were poor and always seemed sad and lonely. Christmas morning I got my necklace, and my cousin got all kinds of stuff. It was from my grandmother and my parents and me and from her mother, but it was everything she wanted and more. She was so happy. I'll never forget it.

"I knew immediately my necklace was from Santa. And though otherwise I got only about half what my cousin got, I wasn't even jealous. I was thrilled for her. That told me something. I was a regular kid. I could have been upset. But the necklace made up for that. And the fact that Santa had somehow made everyone give her what she wanted, well, that proved what I had believed all along. He was real, no matter what my friends, or even my cousin, said. Everyone else quit believing in Santa Claus when they were six or seven. Not me. I always did, and after that Christmas of 1975 I always will."

Tom stared at her. "What can I do?"

"Believe me."

"Short of that."

"You're calling me a liar?"

"I'm getting the picture. I'd rather not believe you actually believe this, but if that's what you're saying—"

"It's all I've been trying to tell you."

"All right. I believe you believe this."

"I want you to still love me."

"I always will, Noella. I want to help."

"You think I need a shrink."

Noella hadn't dared hope Tom would agree or take it in stride. She felt his pity. "I hoped because you loved me that I could risk telling you," she said. "You deserved to know."

"I don't know what to say."

"Yes, you do."

"That I still love you? Of course I do."

"Say it."

"I do."

"Say the words."

"Noella, don't do this. We don't badger each other semantically. I've never cared about anyone the way I—"

"You can't tell me. You can't say, 'I love you.' "

MUCH AS TOM wanted to say what she wanted to hear, he could not. "Do *you* still love *me?*" he asked.

"With all my heart."

"I appreciate that," he said.

"Well, you're welcome," she said. "I'm sorry we won't be doing business with your company, ma'am, but I appreciate your interest."

"Noella."

"Don't talk to me like a column subject."

"You can imagine how this hits me," he said. "I—"

"I've imagined it for months."

Tom wanted to hold her. Neither moved.

"Do you want your ring back?" she said suddenly.

"Why would you say that?"

"Answer a simple question."

"I don't want to do anything rash, Noella."

"Regardless, I wouldn't want to wear your ring if you couldn't accept me the way I am."

"Don't push this right now, Noella. I'm not going to just walk away from you."

"This doesn't add up for you, Tom, right? It can't."

Noella slipped off her diamond.

"Don't do that," he said.

"It's only fair. It wouldn't work."

She held it out to him.

"Please," he said. "Keep it and think about this."

NOELLA COULDN'T FIND the lining behind this cloud. Heartbroken as she was, she felt for Tom. He was right. It was sudden. Likely they both were in shock. There was no sense prolonging the discomfort. She slipped the ring into her pocket. "Can I have a hug?" she said.

In spite of everything, she was warmed by the

enthusiasm of his embrace. She sensed his longing. They had seemed perfect for each other, had come through so much. Destiny wasn't all it was cracked up to be.

She pulled away, crying, and saw his tears. "I'm sorry, Tom," she said. "I'm so sorry."

"You're not dumping me this easily," he said.

TOM FELT AS if he were watching a stranger walk out of his life. She gave him her fluttery wave, and he waited until she was in the elevator before he left. He pulled out of the parking lot, took a right, and pulled over on the deserted street. He opened the door and rolled out, falling to his knees in the snow. He pitched onto his face and sobbed.

NOELLA TOOK OFF her coat and let it slide to the floor. Suddenly weary, she could hardly move. She kicked off her shoes and padded to bed. She lay atop the covers in her clothes and cried herself to sleep.

TWELVE

A ll-Night Flight

TOM WAS FAMILIAR with phantom pain, the malady of amputees. He felt as if his heart had been torn from him.

His routine, his every thought, had revolved around Noella. The very thought of her name wounded him. When would he call her, see her, meet her, touch her, kiss her?

Every solution seemed futile. He loved her. He wanted her. He could not remove her picture from his desk. For a week he sat staring at it, trying to work, sleepwalking through his days.

Writing was impossible. Tom rummaged through his files, looking for stuff that could be tweaked into acceptable columns. He had a couple of fail-safe pieces in case he fell ill or was stranded, but he had never created a real backlog, believing his column had to reflect immediacy.

It was all he could do to manufacture half-timely leads and fresh transitions before he was paralyzed again with grief. The thought of getting out, of scouring the city for his kind of column, repulsed him. Everything repulsed him.

Like the cynic of old, Tom snapped at everyone, suspected everything. His appetite was gone. Even his car reminded him of Noella. On Sunday, December 13, he came to the end of his reserves. He felt himself reverting to the person he had grown to hate. He didn't want to be that person again, yet his negative worldview had been confirmed in spades. The best thing that had ever happened to him was now in ashes.

Tom could not keep himself from calling Noella. He got her answering machine. "Hi, it's Tom. I just wanted to tell you that I miss you and that I care deeply for you. Call me."

He hated his inability to do anything. If this were just a misunderstanding, he would take charge. He would not allow himself to lose her over something he had said or done. But she had made clear that Santa came with the package, and unless Tom could accept that, he and Noella were nowhere.

The next day Tom was greeted by E-mail from the boss. "Come see me as soon as you get a minute. Walt." Tom assumed the worst. He might be able to slip a few mediocre columns past the editors and even the readers, but he couldn't fool Mathes. Walt was the one who had recognized his ability, who championed him to the brass and to the syndicate.

DEVASTATED, NOELLA HAD called in sick on the eighth and ninth, sent a message to her classes on the tenth saying they could study independently that day, then gave them Friday, the eleventh, off as her Christmas gift. They left for the holidays.

She received a nasty phone message from her department chair, Dr. Connie Ng. "We don't write our own schedules here. If you have an emergency, you'll find me more than accommodating. I can't help but wonder whether you simply sliced yourself a bigger piece of the holiday pie than your tenure warrants. Better save some days for your honeymoon."

Sue Beaker had smelled a rat. After classes Friday

she had driven to Noella's and talked her way in. Noella was grateful for Sue's persistence, but she wasn't ready to tell her the truth. Still in her robe in the middle of the day, she had trouble maintaining eye contact. "We broke up. You were right. Oil and water."

"Did he do something, say something?"

Noella waved her off. "I'm just a dreamer, you know, head in the stars and all that."

"He dumped you for being more positive than he is?"

"It was my decision, Sue. It wouldn't have worked. I'm sanguine. He's—"

"Oh, stop with that. You're the best thing that ever happened to him, and if that didn't make him a more positive person—"

"I tried to make him something he wasn't."

"A man with half a brain would change for you, Noella. One day he'll realize—"

"Sue, I need you not to think ill of Tom. I know you mean well, but I loved him as I've never loved anyone. I don't hate him. I miss him. Support me, but don't shoot at him."

Sue sighed. "Okay, but your enemies are my—"

"Tom will never be an enemy."

Sue cautioned Noella against becoming a recluse, "even over the holidays. It's not healthy to hide when you're hurting."

Noella nodded, but she couldn't imagine facing the world yet.

That Monday, the fourteenth, her mother called and left a message. "Are you and Tom joining us Christmas Eve? Plan on staying over."

Noella called her back and asked if she and Grandmother were open for company the next night. "It'll just be me."

"Anything wrong?"

"We'll talk when I get there."

TOM STEPPED INTO Walt's office. Rufus Young was sitting in a side chair.

"I invited him," Walt said. "Hope you don't mind."

"Call it intervention therapy," Rufus said. "How ya doin', Dout'?"

Tom reluctantly sat. "You both know I don't like surprises. What is this? Am I getting fired?"

"That would be brilliant," Walt said. "Make our superstar a free agent."

"Cut the flattery, Walt. What requires a chaperon?"

"If you'd be more comfortable without him—" Walt began, but Tom cut him off.

"If you think I need a friend, there's nobody I'd rather have here. Now let's have it."

"All right, Tom," Walt said. "What's wrong? Don't look at me like you don't know what I'm talking about. You think I don't recognize filler pieces? You've been lazy. Need a break, take a break, but don't take it on the job."

"You're right. I'll get back in gear."

"That's it?" Walt said. "You caught me napping but I'm awake now?"

"What do you want to hear?"

"We want to know what's up, man," Rufus said. "If this was a pattern, okay. But this is the crap pulled by amateurs. You don't coast. And you don't ignore me. So, what's happening? Something with Noella?"

"We broke up."

Rufus and Walt glanced at each other. "Didn't I tell you?" Rufus said.

"Congratulations, Rufus. You win a bet or something?"

"I knew it had to be serious."

"Well, thanks for acknowledging that," Tom said.

"I loved that woman," Rufus said. "You wanna talk about it?"

"No."

"Your privilege," Walt said. "Want some time off?"

Tom knew the paper and the syndicate counted on his stuff, particularly in December. "I might take you up on that in January," he said.

"How's your Christmas piece coming?"

"I'll come up with something."

Walt did not respond. Tom was suspicious.

"What?" Tom said. "You want somebody else to do it?"

"It isn't that."

"What then?"

"Would you consider broadening your horizon this year? The syndicate is suggesting something a little less—"

"Local, yeah, I know. So, send me somewhere. I could use a diversion."

"Name it. Do a Bob Greene. Take a road trip. Fly somewhere."

"You still want humbug?"

"I never wanted humbug. Do I get a choice?"

"I don't need to be more depressed. There's this

guy, friend of Rufus's, raising three kids by himself on the South Side. I—"

"That's still Chicago, Tom. Do that for your regular column, but go somewhere for the Christmas piece. Anywhere."

Tom promised to think about it.

"And do lunch with me one of these days," Rufus said as they left.

Tom looked at his watch. "How about now?"

"As long as we get out of here," Rufus said.

They went to Hunan's nearby.

"You usually love this stuff," Rufus said. "You're gonna need help if you keep picking at it."

Tom shoved his plate toward Rufus, who ate it all.

"Any chance of getting back with Noella?"

Tom shook his head. "Miles apart."

"Love was good for you."

"Don't I know it."

"Can't work it out?"

"She's totally into fantasy, Rufe. Loves the whole Christmas thing."

"You do too, down deep."

"I'd let her have fun with it, but she takes it too far."

"You're a true cynic."

Rufus dabbed his mouth with a napkin and swallowed the rest of his Coke. "Wonder where all that stuff got started. Almost every continent has some kind of Christmas tradition with a character that brings gifts for everybody." He laughed as they rose to leave. "Even the North Pole!"

Tom wished he could find something to laugh about.

TUESDAY NIGHT WAS hard for Noella. She wanted her mother and grandmother to resign themselves to the end of her relationship with Tom.

"Dang it!" Grandmother said. "I liked that boy! I told him you had your head in the stars, but I thought he liked that about you."

"Only to a point."

"Well, when you *do* find a husband—"

"I don't want a husband if it's not Tom."

"You'll change your mind," her mother said. "Time heals."

Noella couldn't imagine.

TOM SPENT WEDNESDAY morning, the sixteenth, on the Internet downloading everything he could find on the origins of Christmas traditions. He was intrigued to find that the idea of exchanging gifts on a special winter day predated Christmas. The idea of Santa Claus stemmed from legends about a real person. Saint Nicholas, born in the 300s A.D. in what is now Turkey.

Just before noon Tom asked to see Walt again. "I've got an idea," he said.

"Uh-oh."

"If Media Services doesn't want to kick in to get me to Germany, I'll pay the difference."

"Germany?"

"The Black Forest. I want to do a piece on how one of the oldest Christmas traditions is holding up in the area where it began."

"Kris Kringle. Father Christmas. That stuff?"

Tom nodded. "Kringle. Father Christmas is English."

"Researching already? Talk about writing against type."

"I'm not up to bashing Christmas this year. I want to interview people in the Black Forest. Kris Kringle is one of the traditions that grew out of the true story of Saint Nicholas. Ever heard it?"

"Can't say that I have," Walt said, "unless you're talking about that 'Night Before Christmas' poem."

"Obviously that's fiction, but the real Saint

Nicholas was said to have helped a poor nobleman. No one would marry the man's three daughters because they had no dowries. The story goes that Nicholas tossed three bags of coins through a window in the man's house so the daughters would have something to take into their marriages."

"Save it for your feature, Tom. The sun may not come up the day we run a warm and fuzzy Christmas piece by you, but I say go for it."

After lunch the *Tribune*'s travel agency told Tom it could get him on a 4:30 P.M. flight to Frankfurt for around two thousand dollars.

Traveling typically light, Tom studied his raft of research on the long trip. He decided that if this story proved popular, he might do his research in Holland next year. The people of the Netherlands particularly loved the Saint Nicholas legend. He read that the first Dutch settlers in the United States had spoken of Saint Nicholas and that English-speaking children had picked up the Dutch name Sinterklaas. It eventually became Santy Claus and then Santa Claus.

Tom learned that while other cultures had their own legendary figures, when Washington Irving described Saint Nick in a story in the 1800s, the modern version of Santa came into view. The poem Walt had referred to actually appeared in a newspaper first, the *Troy Sentinel*, in 1823. Forty years later a *Harper's Weekly* cartoonist sketched Santa on the basis of those earlier writings.

Tom discovered that a northern Germany legend says Christmas Man delivers presents. Kris Kringle is southern Germany's version of Santa.

Tom arrived in Germany at 8:00 the next morning, 1:00 A.M. Chicago time, following a rich journalistic tradition to update the Santa myth. He had agreed to keep in touch with Walt and also make his deadlines via E-mail. Holed up at the Frankfurt Main Hilton, he wanted to stay awake and fight off jet lag. He rapped out a column about his plans and added a note to Walt that he was booked on a midday flight to Stuttgart. Tom would look for a flight to the Black Forest. Interviewing the locals to see what had become of the ancient legend, he hoped, would give him enough material to carry him through the end of the year.

THIRTEEN

Mayday!

NOELLA SLEPT THROUGH the night for the first time since the breakup and awoke early Thursday. Her goal was somehow to endure the days of sharpest pain and limp into the postholiday term with renewed enthusiasm for her students. She had long been a goal-oriented person. If she wrote and sold one more article before the end of the year, she would have fulfilled her annual objectives. Still she ached, but she was through wallowing.

Noella called the *Tribune* and left a message for Rufus Young. "Remind me of the name of the single father you recommended to Tom. I'd ask Tom, but I'm sure you know that would be difficult for both of us just now."

At eight that morning Rufus returned her call. "Hey, girl," he said. "You all right?"

"I'm okay."

"Can I help you two get back together somehow?"

"Is that what he wants?"

"It's what you both want, and you know it."

"It'll have to be his choice, Rufus."

"He said this was your decision."

"There's a prerequisite to my changing my mind."

"And it's all on him and none of my business?"

"Is he all right?"

"No."

"Why? What?"

"He's hurting. You know he's out of the country."

"I didn't know."

"Probably in Germany by now. On assignment."

"Wow." She wanted details but didn't want it to get back that she was asking.

Rufus gave her Robert Taylor's name.

"I could use a good photographer."

They agreed on six o'clock. He would clear it with Taylor, and Noella would pick up Rufus in the parking garage near the *Tribune*. She felt half healthy for the first time in days. Not whole, but she was ready to do something.

Tom WANTED TO stay awake until a normal bedtime, hoping to acclimate as soon as possible. He was to return to Chicago the following Monday, and he didn't want his brief stay to be one long battle to stay awake during the day and asleep at night.

At 2:00 P.M. Germany time, Tom negotiated with an impatient-looking charter pilot at the Stuttgart airport. He enlisted a young woman at the Lufthansa counter to interpret.

She said, "He says he's taking two men from a Canadian printing company and delivering a press to Sankt Georgen im Schwarzwald. Schwarzwald is Black Forest. It will be tight, though, because—"

"I don't mind. Where is this Sankt whatever?"

"South, near the Brigach River, not far from Switzerland."

"Any idea whether there would be any sources of Christmas tradition, Kris Kringle–type stuff in that area?"

"Probably," she said. "He says you would have to be weighed, and your luggage."

"This is all I have. The one bag. Can't be more than two hundred pounds, me included."

The pilot insisted on an exact figure. They found a scale, and Tom proved right. He and his bag totaled just over the metric equivalent of 195 pounds. The pilot scribbled in a small spiral notebook, then quoted a figure.

"That's what it cost me to get here from Frankfurt," he said. The interpreter shrugged, and the pilot looked resolute.

"He wants payment now and will take off in two hours."

"Tell him I wasn't born yesterday. I'll pay when I get on the plane."

Fortunately one of the Canadians knew German. He communicated with the pilot as they hoisted the heavy printing press into the fuselage behind the seats. The two-engine plane was a four-seater, and Tom understood why the pilot had spent so much time ciphering. "Ask him how close we are to maximum weight," Tom said to the taller of the Canadians.

"He says we're fine," the man said. "Good news for you. You're the Jonah."

"I'm sorry?"

"If we're overweight, you're out. Last man in, first one out."

"Sounds fair. But we're okay?"

"We'd better be. Nobody wants to be lost in that forest."

"It's not the Black Forest of old, you know," the other Canadian said. "Much of it was destroyed in World War Two. It's been reforested, mostly in neat rows."

"We don't need to know that unless we wind up in the forest," the tall one said, laughing. Tom was too tired to smile. And he didn't like the concern on the pilot's face.

"How long is this flight?" Tom said.

"Less than an hour."

The Canadians took the two back seats. Tom sat next to the pilot and found the excitement of takeoff in a small plane enough to keep him awake temporarily. When they finally lumbered into the air, the pilot smiled and said something. The Canadian said, "He says the rest is easy."

The Canadians talked loudly for a few minutes, trying to make themselves heard over the engines. Surprised at how drafty the plane felt, Tom was glad he had kept his coat on. His big, soft bag lay in his lap. The drone of the engines and chatter he could no longer decipher lulled him. His eyes grew heavy, his head began to bob, and soon he laid his arms over the bag, rested his forehead in the crook of his elbow, and fell into a deep sleep.

The sun was creeping behind the trees when Tom awoke. What had awakened him? A bounce, a dip, something. He had felt it in his stomach but wanted nothing more than to remain dead to the world. Something was golden about stolen moments of sleep in incongruous places when you could hardly stay awake anyway.

Tom was surprised at how quickly the sky had grown dark. His lids fluttered, and his head felt leaden, but the plane seemed to be struggling. Knowing the pilot didn't understand him anyway, he said, "Everything okay?" The man did not acknowledge him. Tom looked behind him. One of the Canadians slept. The other seemed unconcerned.

Tom knew little about aviation, but he knew what an altimeter was. This one showed they were descending fast. The pilot worked to maintain an even keel. Tom stole another glance back. The Canadian looked at his watch. "Quick trip," he said, and reached to rouse his friend. "We made good time."

Tom knew better. He peered down on miles of snow and trees. The pilot feathered the controls. Tom had no idea what had gone wrong. Were they too heavy? The nose dipped. The pilot yanked back on the stick. The Canadians shouted as the printing press slammed into their seats. The pilot reached for the radio. "Mayday!" he called out. "Mayday! Schwarzwald! Black Forest! Mayday!"

Tom wished he would forget the radio and concentrate on the controls. The right engine sputtered. The pilot dropped the microphone and fought for control. "Keep the nose up!" came from the back. "Head first and we're dead!" Tom feared the pilot knew only enough English to communicate with towers.

Tom's body was alive, buzzing with adrenaline. The pilot and the other two cried the wails of the doomed. Tom hugged his bag tighter as the left engine died. The nose dipped; the pilot fought gravity; trees came into view. Tom battled the urge to shut his eyes against the inevitable. Believing he was about to die, he still didn't want to miss a thing.

The pilot, looking as if he'd rather be standing, leaned this way and that, futilely trying to keep the dead bird airborne. A last yank on the stick allowed the nose to clear the top branches. Their only hope was that the boughs might keep them level before they plunged through the trees.

Noella, I love you with all my heart, Tom said silently, *and I always will.*

The left wing brushed first, slowing the plane so quickly that the right side swung violently around like a carnival ride. The wings sheared off as the nose slammed into a tree high in the middle of a grove. The fuselage flipped end over end, the printing press driving the left rear seat into the back of the pilot's seat. Tom covered his face in case he flew through the windshield but saw everything on the other side of the plane driven out—passenger, pilot, seats, controls, and all. What was left of the plane broke apart and cartwheeled, branches rustling past on what seemed an interminable drop. *Noella, Noella,* Tom thought. Soon he was dreaming.

Though he felt both warm and cold, Tom enjoyed a deep sleep. He dreamed of Noella. They ran in deep snow. She turned, smiling. But he couldn't catch her. Now he was alone. Far from home. Something had happened. Loud noises. Fear. A crash. But he was dreaming. And he knew it. All a dream. His body willed him to wake up. He fought it. So comfortable. He just wanted to sleep.

Tom had been holding something. His bag. He didn't want to open his eyes to find it. His hands were cold. His side was cold. He tucked his hands beneath his chin and brought his knees up. Just a few more minutes of sleep, beautiful sleep. He was outdoors. Dreaming. So, so comfortable.

Liquid. He lay in liquid. His cheek, his temple, his ear, wet. No pain. Deep breathing gave way to panting, gasping. His heart raced. A nightmare? He shuddered, his body trembling like a dried leaf in the wind. Why couldn't he stay asleep?

Tom fought to calm down, to find a better dream. But he lost the battle with his insistent body. He forced his eyes open. His right eye was cloudy. Faint shafts of sunlight retreated. Tom stared at his knees. He was still in his seat, belt fastened. Behind him lay one of the Canadians, clearly dead, neck broken. The plane was now just sheets of twisted metal. Fifty feet ahead, at the base of a tree, lay the bodies of the pilot and the other passenger. Tom struggled with his seat belt. If he was alive, he had to do something.

FOURTEEN

Dead Man's Watch

HOW LONG HAD Tom lain in the snow, still belted to his seat? There was no way to gauge how far they had come before the crash. Was he walking distance from civilization? His right hand was asleep beneath him. He lifted his left hand to look at his watch in the twilight. No watch. He planted a foot to sit up but had to unstrap first. He dug for the buckle, and pain raked his ribs.

Tom leaned hard on his elbow and arched his back. With the buckle finally unlatched, he rolled right, and the seat fell away. He pushed with his right foot and turned onto his back. The sky was just dark enough to reveal a few stars. *Move,* he told himself. Move or die in the middle of nowhere.

Tom rolled his ankles. The right was already swelling. He tried lifting his knees. Only the left would move. He pivoted his pelvis gently, ruling out a fracture. His right hand had circulation now. He knew he had rib damage, but though his heart raced and he panted, he sensed no damage to his cardiopulmonary system. He tried to calm himself, to regulate his breathing. He was concerned but not scared. Yet. Fear would come if he could not move.

His hands raw and cold, he planted them in the snow and tried to sit up. How bad was the right? He lifted it, and his elbow throbbed. It would take no pressure. He had no choice. No way he could push off with it. He would have to play hurt, like any team player. The truth washed over him. Unless someone else had survived and was able to help, he could die. His only chance was to move.

Marshaling every reserve, Tom gritted his teeth, rolled left, and, with a scream that terrified him, sat up. His head wobbled. His collarbone was certainly cracked. He was sweating profusely. How long before hypothermia did him in?

He shut his eyes to keep the darkening landscape from whirling. He set his palms in the snow again to steady himself. *Think! Assess your injuries. Know what you have to work with.*

Right ankle swelling. Right knee swelling. Right elbow at least deeply bruised. Left ribs cracked. Left collarbone cracked. He wiped his right temple and cheek. Blood. Tom had to know the source. He rubbed his hand on his coat to dry and warm it, then flexed his fingers. He carefully felt the right side of his face. There it was, a deep laceration on his ear. He forced himself to breathe steadily and relax. The injury to his ear was good news. It would not gush like a scalp wound.

Nothing serious broken, he guessed. No wound deep enough to bleed him out. Directly behind him was the body of the tall Canadian who had sat behind him on the plane and been the interpreter. He found the man's wallet. His family would want something personal. There was no wedding ring. His watch was expensive, but it had been smashed.

Tom centered his weight over his good leg and forced himself to stand. As he teetered, he gingerly put a little weight on his swollen leg. No go. He hopped, trying to keep his balance, his neck shooting daggers to his brain. The landscape swirled, and he felt every injury as he flopped onto his back.

Tom was exhausted and dizzy, and his heart and lungs worked overtime again. Now he was mad and determined. His goal was a tree ten feet ahead. Grunting, then roaring against the pain, he again rolled to his side, sat up, got that left leg under him, and rose. He lurched, aiming for the tree. At the last second, as Tom tried to get his left arm around the trunk, he slipped and had to turn his head to keep his face from taking the brunt of the collision. He grabbed branches and pulled himself up, realizing he had fresh scrapes, this time from pine needles, on his right cheek. A flimsy branch supported him as he tried to collect himself.

His only chance was to keep from panicking, use his uninjured limbs to move, and find help.

What were the chances the radio still worked? The control panel had flown out with the other Canadian, the pilot, and the printing press. The bodies were deeper into the trees. The panel had to be close. It was darker there and would soon be pitch.

Tom tried to walk, holding branches as he moved between trees. The best he could do was hop. How would he get anywhere in the open? He spent more than ten minutes making his way to the pilot. Tom vainly felt for a pulse and tried not to look at the man, who had been crushed beyond recognition. Strangely, his watch was still running. Tom slipped it off. If he survived, he would return it to the man's family.

He looked for other personal items that might mean something to the pilot's loved ones. He removed a wedding ring, no easy task because the fingers were swollen. The other body had also been crushed and torn nearly in two. Tom could not find a wallet, but he removed an ID bracelet that read "M.K." He found gloves in the ripped jacket.

The control panel had been obliterated, the radio a mass of broken wires and a chassis beyond repair. Besides, there was no power source, and Tom wouldn't know where to begin looking for the battery.

He needed to rest. He lowered himself slowly but soon felt the wet cold through his pants. Tom had to be smart. Wet and cold were dangerous. If he had to be in the elements long, he would need a fire and dry clothes. He searched for emergency provisions and found only a packet containing two flares. He would save one in case he heard a search plane. The pilot had transmitted the mayday and specified the Black Forest. Unfortunately the forest was huge, and the wreckage not likely visible from the air. Tom would use the other flare to start a fire.

A hole in the control panel indicated where the compass had been. Tom knew too little about the positions of the stars to get far. He found the compass just before the forest turned black. The night was clear, and the sky bright, but Tom was suddenly overwhelmed with fatigue and grief. He didn't know these men, but he hated leaving their bodies to the elements. He could only hope a rescue team would arrive soon enough to dispose of the bodies appropriately.

Tom searched for food and found not even a candy bar. They all believed they would be on the ground less than an hour after takeoff. And they were. How long since he had slept? He had napped on the plane, but he needed a full night's sleep and didn't know whether he'd ever see a bed again.

Tom was a pragmatist. He would exercise his few options. A map at the Stuttgart airport had shown how desolate the Black Forest was, a tremendous amalgam of trees and mountains. The few towns appeared tiny and impossible to reach on foot. Especially one foot.

Tom decided they had flown at least halfway to Sankt Georgen near the Brigach River, more than fifty miles southwest of Stuttgart. Assuming the pilot had taken them on a straight line, Tom would continue southwest and hope the city was reachable.

His right ankle could take no weight. His knee wasn't much better, but he could crawl. Able to push off the inside of his knee, he kept his foot elevated as much as possible. Slowly, painfully, after an hour of cold, wet, exhausting crawling, he had gone only a few hundred yards.

Tom was moving uphill. He pushed on, gloves sodden, knees burning with the wet cold. Crawling, virtually with one hand, seemed a stubborn last gasp. In the moonlight ahead he saw a board attached to a post. Something to shoot for. Tired. So tired.

Tom stopped only when he sensed he was overloading his heart. He waited until his pulse dipped, peeked at the compass, and pressed on. When he finally reached the rustic sign, he found a direction marker, no kilometer markings, just arrows and names. Rottweil was behind him. Dunningen was to the west. Neither meant anything to him. He stored them in his mind, so he could tell authorities where to locate the bodies. An hour later he heard river sounds. If that was the Brigach, there was a sliver of hope. He would follow it west toward Sankt Georgen, and only death would keep him from getting there. His teeth chattered; his aching bones and muscles cried out. His pain had gone from local to global. It was as if he *were* the pain, his wasted body a clumsy clump of frozen tissue, snailing through the snow.

IT WAS MIDAFTERNOON in Chicago. Noella sat jotting notes, planning her interview with Robert Taylor. Tom had told her the basics, but she wanted to concentrate on the children, the essence of being raised in a tough neighborhood by a single father. She couldn't share the experience with Tom, couldn't bounce ideas off him. The break had been her choice, yet it was hard. She missed him. Missed his wit, his mind, his voice.

Now she was off track. She couldn't think of anything but what she missed about Tom. His hands. His smile. His eyes. His touch. His lips. She folded her arms across her stomach, doubling over with the pain. *What have I done?* How easy it would be to renounce her belief and admit she'd come to her senses. Everybody past the age of seven knew there was no Santa Claus. She whispered, trying the idea on for size. "Tom," she said to the empty room, "I don't know what I was thinking. I'm over it. Let's try again."

It had been the only issue between them. Could she renege? Could she mean it?

She fingered the medallion.

No.

Effort made Tom ravenous. Pausing to conserve strength was hopeless. Every second he delayed increased the odds against him. He held snow in his hands, hoping it would melt so he could drink the water. But his hands served as an igloo that kept the snow from melting. He ate it.

Tom soon came to the end of his strength. The river was over the next rise. He wanted to follow it west, he hoped to Sankt Georgen. But his body gave out. He dropped face first and lay in the snow several minutes. The wind kicked up. If he could just gather something to burn, he could warm up. Maybe fate would smile on him, and someone would notice the fire from the air or from a nearby town.

Tom crawled into a large grove of trees, where he found handfuls of dry foliage. He set the pile out of the wind and lit it with a flare. The twigs burst into flames, and he hurled the flare out in the open, just in case. Soaked through, he tried to think of something else to burn.

Tom sat painfully cross-legged before his fire and warmed his hands. He looked at the borrowed watch, guessing it would read four in the morning. It was a few minutes past midnight. He put his face as close to the flame as he dared. Rest. He needed rest. He leaned on his good elbow, close to the fire. He closed his eyes for an instant, just to relax.

Tom could feel his fire dying, yet he didn't have the energy to fuel it. When it was out, he would start again, heading west to follow the river. His breathing became regular and deep.

In the tree above him he made out a kindly lined face with a generous nose, big ears, a floppy hat, and slippered feet dangling. He sat up. An elf? And there were others! All smiling, nodding, urging him on. He felt like running, but could he? His clothes felt dry, yet they were the clothes of a small boy. Tom was nine again, separated from his parents and scared. Where was everybody?

Go! he told himself. *Go! Go!* But he could not move. He wanted to cry out for his mother, but he could not speak. The kindly elves in the trees disappeared as quickly as they had appeared. He was alone again, small and paralyzed in the snow.

ROBERT TAYLOR AND Rufus chatted in the living room while Noella joined the Taylor children at the kitchen table. The boys, David and Corrie, wouldn't look at her while showing off. They bragged about sports and their grades. Noella was drawn to Betsy, meticulously writing a letter on lined paper in large, cursive characters. Her tongue matched her strokes.

"Who are you writing to?" Noella said.

"Santa."

"Santa!" the boys parroted. "Make-believe! Make-believe!"

"Huh-uh," Betsy singsonged as she continued. "Comin' at Christmas."

The boys laughed so hard their dad shushed them from the other room. Noella sat next to Betsy. "Is it private?"

Betsy shook her head.

Noella read: "Dear Santa: My big brothers say your not real, but I know you are. I dont have a list of what I want for Crismas because my dad alreddy knows and he gets us whatever he can. He thinks you are not real too. My mom is ded. How are you? All I want for

Crismas is rest for my dad. He works to hard and takes care of us to. He say hes going to get extra days off over the holly days. So were all going to promis to be quite and let him sleep. Thats what I want. Love Betsy from Chicago."

Noella's lips quivered. "Santa answers that kind of letter, honey. I wrote him when I was little."

"What did he bring you?"

Noella showed her the necklace.

"Did you ask for it?"

"No."

"I bet your daddy got you that."

"It was Santa."

"Nuh-uh. Not if you didn't ask for it."

TOM STOOD, SUDDENLY full-grown again. Along the riverbank a neon sign told him the Frankfurt airport was one mile ahead, an exit for Chicago two miles. He staggered north, and there was Noella on an overpass with the elves in Santa's sleigh, smiling, waving, showing him, showing everyone her ring. And her necklace.

He ran past cars and trucks and buses that couldn't seem to navigate the icy exit ramp. He waited at a red light as Noella gazed lovingly from across the street. She opened her arms when the light changed, but now the ramp was too steep, the footing treacherous. Cars honked. A bus shouldered by, eclipsing the sleigh. When it passed, she and the sleigh were gone.

Tom spun and saw her behind him, going down the ramp the wrong way, against traffic. He called to her. She looked back and smiled and beckoned him. He feared falling on the ice, but he tried anyway. He couldn't move. Couldn't move.

"Noella!" he called. And the sound woke him.

Tom struggled to sit up in the blackness, cold, wet, desolate, and sad as he had ever been. He crawled into the clearing between the trees and the river and squinted at the dead man's watch in the starlight. It was three o'clock in the morning, and he feared he was dying.

FIFTEEN

Twilight Rescue

HUGE FLAKES BLINDED Tom as he crawled, and he didn't trust his judgment. Was he dreaming? Hallucinating? Remembering the snowstorm that hit Chicago? It would be just like Mother Nature to pelt him with the same flakes. No two alike? They were probably all duplicates!

Worse, a search plane might spot the wreckage but not his trail. This was a waste. Why die miserable when you could curl up and get warm? Tom knew he would sleep, maybe luck out with a dream that stayed happy until he had time to die.

His mind was a jumble, his leaden limbs continuing to move. If by some incredible chance he got out of this, he was going straight to Noella. He'd tell her he believed in Santa Claus with all his heart. If all he had to do was abide that fib for the rest of his life, it was a small price to marry the woman of his dreams.

Tom awoke again after dreaming he had been crawling through the desert in shorts and dress shoes. Oases. Mirages. How long had he been out this time? He looked at the watch. Nearly an hour. Hypothermia loomed. How long could he hold out, saving that last flare for a plane?

He talked to himself aloud, knowing his mind would go before his body did. He smacked himself in the face with his good hand, then again, hard. "Stay awake! Keep moving! You've never been a quitter! Your mind has been your strength. Think of the stories you can write from this!"

That made him laugh, but the laugh scared him. What if he was found and dragged off to an asylum? He pitched into the snow to rest a moment. Just a moment. A plane! He sat up and dug through his pockets for the flare. The plane was loud, now louder. Now overhead! He ripped his pocket pulling the flare free, willed his tender fingers to rip off the paper cover, pop the top, and strike the flint. Nothing. Again. Nothing. He awoke. A dream. All a dream. Everything ethereal.

He swore and felt his pocket. The flare was still

there. He crawled on, fighting sobs at the hopelessness of it all.

NOELLA SAT IN her bedroom writing thank-you notes to Robert Taylor and each of the Taylor kids. Might she and Tom have had children? She would have raised them with love and a sense of security. How she missed Tom!

On a scale of one to one hundred, she and Tom were a ninety-nine. She had ended their relationship for a one percent problem. Could she grant him a waiver on one issue? Shouldn't they at least discuss it? If nothing else, that would give her an excuse to see Tom. She would not hold him or kiss him or tell him she loved him. But she could see him.

TOM STILL MOVED his limbs, but they no longer propelled his body. He feared it was over. He passed out every few moments. He pinched himself, hoping he was only dreaming. His body was mercifully numb. He willed himself into a crawling position, but he could not move. He would not surrender to a nap that might kill him. Could he hold out till dawn, till a plane might find him there, walking distance from the river?

Tom feared rescuers would find a frozen corpse. It had come down to breathing or quitting, no easy decision anymore. He was not ready to sacrifice his chance, slim though it was, for a life with Noella. He owed it to himself to go out kicking and screaming. He would not volunteer to die.

At nine in the morning Noella called Sue Beaker. "I need to talk," she said. "But I need a sacred promise of confidentiality."

"Sure, hon, what's up?"

"That's not much of a promise. This requires a face-to-face. Right now."

"You're pregnant!"

"Seriously, Sue, I need you. And don't tell even Bernie. This is something I've never told anyone but Tom."

Tom heard mechanical racket over the sounds of the river. Where was it coming from? Delirious, he worried he was hallucinating again. He bit his lip. It hurt. "Stay with me, Tom," he said aloud.

He hollered for help, but his voice was too weak to

carry. If only he could stand, he could see farther. He hoisted himself one more time, grimacing. To the west and farther north of the river, he saw lights. Somehow he had to muster the strength to get to that light and that sound. And, he hoped, to people.

NOELLA MET SUE at the Evanston library and told her everything.

"Sometimes I wish I could return to childhood too, Noella. But you're crazy for letting this come between you and Tom. And I didn't even like him that much!"

"Thanks."

"You deserve the truth. Be glad I'm still your friend."

"Are you?"

"A little shell-shocked, but yes. Now insist on seeing him immediately. This is not worth losing him over. Jeez, Noella. You really know how to screw things up."

TOM ROCKED UP onto his hands and knees, nearly fainting from the pain. He would crawl as fast as he could, get someone's attention, or die trying. The pain in his elbow brought tears to his eyes. His leg was less a problem, it was so cold and numb. It was if he were dragging a frozen log, but he willed that knee to bend. Tom sucked air. Yelling from the pain, he charged through the snow. He feared that if he stopped, he was finished.

When he had covered half the distance to the light and noise, he stopped and screamed for help. He saw movement from an opening in an outcropping of rock. Were those heads poking out? He rocked back onto his knees, waving. More movement. More heads, bodies. People!

He had only enough energy to keep breathing. If they ran away, he was dead anyway. It was on them now. He was their responsibility. Tom tumbled forward one last time and passed out.

NOELLA RETURNED TO her apartment just before five. To her horror, her answering machine was jammed with messages.

First: "Hey, Noella, Rufus. You there? Pick up, please. All right. Call me when you get in."

Second: "Me again. Okay, call me at the *Trib*."

Third: "Sorry to keep bugging you. Call as soon as you can."

Fourth: "Noella, I need to hear from you. It's urgent."

Fifth: "Just checking."

Sixth: "I'm going to try you every fifteen minutes. I won't leave any more messages, so if you've got this far on the tape, call me. If it's after five, I'll be in the car."

Noella dialed, hands shaking. "Rufus, it's—"

"Are you home?"

"Yes! Now, what—"

"I'm on my way. I'm almost to the Ike, so I'll be a while. Stay there."

"Tell me what's going on."

"Not on the phone."

"You have to! I'll go crazy!"

"Listen to me, Noella, I need to talk to you in person. Trust me."

"Rufus, please!"

"I'm sorry. Wait for me."

THE SUN WAS low on the horizon when Tom was found. He tried to talk. He wanted to smile. But he worried he was too far gone. What if his body temperature had plummeted so far it was too late to save him? Could these people get a message to the States?

To Noella, to the *Tribune*, to Canada, to the rescue team? He mumbled and tried to force his eyes open. He was on his back on a wooden sled, pulled by people who spoke quickly in what sounded like German.

Tom turned and forced his eyes open. He saw a pickax on a leather tool belt worn by one of the men. He was very short. Tom looked more closely. The man was an adult, middle-aged, and tiny. But he was not a dwarf or a midget. He was a miniature person, perfectly proportioned. *I'm dreaming again,* Tom told himself.

The man smiled and gently pushed Tom back to a supine position. Tom looked the other way and saw another miniature man. *I've got it bad this time,* he thought. He bit his tongue and winced. *I'm even dreaming pain.*

When next he opened his eyes, he was in a bed too small. His legs hung off the end by three feet. It was again the middle of the night. He was hungry. Disoriented. The understatement of the ages. The little men jabbered in their own language as they tended his wounds. Things were happening inside his body. His aching bones vibrated with what felt like music, if music could be felt. Yet when the men were silent, so was the night. No creature noises. No sound of wind.

HE'S DEAD, NOELLA concluded. What else could it be? She paced, watched out the window, sat, and cried. She scolded herself. *Why think the worst? It could be anything. Something happened to Robert Taylor or one of his kids. Tom's been fired. Tried to kill himself. My fault. Snap out of it!*

She put her coat on. She would wait for Rufus at the back door.

THE LITTLE MEN, miners it appeared, followed the lead of one of their own. He spoke soothingly to Tom, though Tom still understood none of it. Whatever they had done to him, he was already feeling better.

Hands had traversed his body, probing. When he groaned, heat or cold was applied, then a wrap. He was fed hot liquid that tasted like tea, sweet as orange juice. No food, and suddenly he didn't crave any. A fire roared in the fireplace at the end of what he now recognized as a dormitory. Saved by a band of tiny miners. Go figure. He sensed their magic ministrations had somehow saved his life and begun his healing.

His clothes had been replaced by an old flannel

nightshirt, incongruously way too big for him. He swam in it and was also covered with three small quilts. One of the men opened a cloth sack to show that his belongings were there: three wallets, a ring, an ID bracelet, a compass, a flare.

Tom wanted to sleep. He let his eyes close, but they popped open again when the men surrounded him and worked together to lift him back onto the sled. "No!" he managed to cry, but they ignored him. The elder tried to soothe him. Tom feared they had done their duty and now worried that this big man might harm them. They were going to put him back where they found him. But he was harmless! He just wanted a phone!

"Not outside again!" he said, thrashing. They tried to calm him, but it was soon unnecessary. Snow blew in when the door opened, and as they dragged the sled noisily across the floor, Tom shook his head and lost consciousness yet again.

NOELLA SAT ON the steps, looking out the glass door to the parking lot. When Rufus slid in, she bounded down and opened the door for him. He looked grave.

"What?" she said.

"Your apartment."

"Just tell me, Rufus!" she shouted, and he embraced her. She sobbed. "He's dead, isn't he?"

"We don't know," he said. "Let's go sit down, and I'll tell you what we do know."

SIXTEEN

"*Wait for Father*"

TOM FELT THE sting of the night air on his face. He came to and smelled animals and manure. The trip from the little dormitory to wherever they were taking him went past a corral. He sat up, and though the men seemed to urge him to lie back down, they looked frightened. None dared touch him.

Beyond low wood rails stood reindeer. *I'm dead,* he decided. Someone ran ahead, and lights came on inside the main house and on the front porch. *I'm still in the snow near the river, broken beyond repair. My dreams have come full circle. How will I know when it's over and that I'll never awaken again?*

The men stopped at stairs that led to a cottage so warm and inviting that Tom felt as if he were in another dimension. It was as if he were writing his own children's story, something that would make him feel safe on a dark night in a home with a volatile father. In this perfect vision, a candle burned in each window, a thatched roof covered the dwelling, and smoke white as clouds billowed lazily from the chimney.

The miners spread out around the sled to hoist Tom to the door. He panicked. Could they manage? Might he tumble out? Should he care? Wasn't this a dream in which he could affect the events? *Let them carry me,* he thought. *I'll roll over and pitch out and float with the chimney smoke to the reindeer.*

As the men set themselves to move, the door flew open. A rosy-cheeked woman in robe, slippers, and nightcap bustled out, whispering in a vibrato that never dropped below high C. "Oh, no, no, no," she sang. "My, my, what has happened? Don't lift him. Wait for Father."

Tom lay back down. He understood her! *I'm inventing scenarios based on snippets of this and that.* Strange, he still felt pain.

The men spoke excitedly to the woman, and still he could not understand them. He sat up. "Excuse me, ma'am. How is it you speak English and the little fellas speak German?"

"Don't excite yourself," she said, pulling her robe tighter under her chin and carefully starting down the steps. "Please lie down. The helpers tell me you've suffered nasty injuries. It fascinates them because we do not endure illness or injury here."

"Why do you speak English and they don't?"

The men helped her down the last couple of steps. She carefully helped Tom lie back down. He was stunned, his senses heightened. *So this is what the end is like?* She smelled of cologne and the smoky cottage. She brought the coziness of the home with her into the weather and warmed him, physically and emotionally.

The woman bent near him. "They speak the language of the place," she said quietly. "We understand each other. Father and I speak a universal language for our kind, so the occasional mortal can understand."

"They understand when I do?"

She smiled and nodded.

"And who is Father?"

"He's on his way," she said. "I woke him when I came out."

"So you're Mother?"

She nodded.

Tom looked at the men. "I'm not *their* mother, no!" she said. They laughed.

If this were a dream, Tom decided, he would see Noella at the top of the stairs, and she would elude him.

"Whose mother are you?" he asked. But before she answered, the men stepped aside, and the front door opened again.

"Kris!" she exulted. "We have a guest, an injured mortal. The helpers have patched him up, but he needs more care."

"Let's have a look," Kris said, and he lumbered down in boots, long johns, and a thick robe. Tom pushed himself up with his good arm. This couldn't be real. Snow-white hair, big beard, twinkly eyes, half glasses low on his nose. A cherry-wood pipe.

Kris put a hand behind Tom's head and another on his chest and lowered him slowly. Tom felt cherished, the musical vibrations surging through him again. "Convinced we're figments of your imagination?" Kris asked.

Tom nodded.

Kris smiled. "Is there a mortal without pride? Your imagination is responsible for only so much of what you see. Tell me, boys," he said, "do we have reindeer tonight?"

They giggled and nodded.

Tom felt a fool. "The reindeer aren't always here?"

"They're here as long as you're here. None with a red nose, however. We've hosted Western mortals before, but none has had the wherewithal to conjure Rudolph."

Tom reeled.

"Let's get you inside," Kris said. "The boys cannot carry you. Give me your good arm."

Standing dizzied Tom, but the big man—who looked fat but proved solid—steadied and all but carried him into the house. Mother followed and gathered blankets from a closet. Kris led Tom to the guest bedroom, just off the living room. Outside the little men chattered as they ran back to their dorm with the sled.

"They spend much of their time in the mines," Kris said. "We owe you a debt of gratitude for providing excitement."

"Don't mention it," Tom said, suddenly uncomfortable with his fantasy.

"Our bedroom is beyond the kitchen," Mother said. "We'll hear if you call for us. You must enjoy this while it lasts. You'll mend quickly and be gone before you know it."

Kris and the Mrs. helped him into a luxurious four-poster bed of mahogany. It featured a marshmallowy comforter and down-filled pillows. Tom ached all over,

but he was also warm and drowsy and felt as if he were
floating on air.

"Is it Kris Kringle then?" Tom said.

"That depends."

"She called you Kris outside."

"Then that makes me Kringle. How you came to
us determines what you hear. Mrs. Kringle called me
by my universal name in our language. Had you come
through France, you'd have heard Père, and she would
be Madame Noël. In Russia you would have heard
Grandfather, and our name would be Frost. In your
homeland she'd have called me Santa."

Tom could not keep his eyes open.

RUFUS OUTLINED THE situation for Noella. "It's after
midnight tomorrow in Germany already. A charter
plane called in a mayday over the Black Forest. Tom
was on that plane. It appears no one survived."

Noella closed her eyes and shuddered, fighting to
keep the truth from invading her mind.

"I'm sorry, dear," Rufus said. "Nothing is confirmed except that the plane crashed and no passenger
has been heard from."

Noella wanted Tom back; that was all there was to it. In the hours since she had decided at least to talk to him about it, she'd determined she would never let anything come between them again. She would admit her fantasy. Santa was a concept, an idea, a legend, a myth.

Not to get to tell him she'd changed her mind was so frustrating Noella thought she would explode. She could not accept that Tom was gone. Time would never heal this wound. She took off her necklace, excused herself, and plodded to her bedroom and tossed it in the back of a dresser drawer.

TOM FELL ASLEEP on his back, hands at his sides. He awoke in that exact position. It was the middle of the afternoon, he guessed, and he must have slept ten hours.

He sat on the edge of the bed, the big nightshirt draped about him. His pain had dulled, and he thought it kind of the fates not to awaken him in the snow of the Black Forest, where he was certain he lay even now, dying or dead of hypothermia.

Tom stood. His leg was still tender, but by holding on to the bed, a dresser, and then the door, he hobbled into the living room. Smells from the kitchen intoxicated him, and Mrs. Kringle called out, "I'm on my way, young man! Back to bed with you!"

She brought him stacks of flapjacks and a creamy fruit mixture that hit him like a narcotic. He fell asleep eating, and when he awoke, it was nighttime again. In the candlelight he saw Kris Kringle at the foot of his bed and smelled the sweet aroma of his pipe. "Sleep or rise," the man said. "I'm ready to talk when you are."

"I'm not really here, am I?" Tom said, his voice reminding him of his childhood, asking his father for something he knew he would not get.

"You're here," Kris said.

"Am I alive?"

"Indeed. But you are mortal after all."

"When does this fantasy end? I have so many questions."

"That's why you're here."

"Where is 'here'? The Black Forest?"

"You came to us through the Black Forest. You could have found me at home or in England, France, Russia, Holland—"

"You're an idea, a spirit."

"I am Santa Claus."

"My former fiancée believes you are real."

"I know her well. A Christmas Eve baby with a lovely name."

"There you are wrong."

"There are few true believers. I know them all."

"She believes you brought her—"

"A platinum pendant bearing her birth date. I crafted it myself."

"Where did you get the platinum?"

"My helpers, you call them elves, mine it."

"There is no platinum in this part of the world. I studied it."

Kris smiled and puffed. "This is Fairyland, my friend. We have been here always. We do not tire. We never age. Time does not pass here. Sunrise and sunset merely provide a framework for our activities. We make gifts, like Noella's."

"But her birthday—"

"December twenty-fourth, 1965."

"It was the twenty-sixth," Tom said.

"A lie or a mistake."

"Not yours?"

"That's not the kind of mistake we'd make."

"Sir, she was born the day after Christmas."

"Begging your pardon," Kris said, " 'twas the night before."

Tom smiled. "You know the poem by that title?"

Santa shook his head. "One begins with that line, but the actual title is 'A Visit from St. Nicholas.'"

"Is it accurate?"

"To a degree."

"How do you do it?"

"It?"

"Visit every home on Christmas Eve."

"Time zones help."

"Seriously."

"I do not visit every home. One doubter will keep me away. I get things to believers, sometimes through skeptics, but I visit only the rare home where belief in me is unanimous."

"But you make exceptions."

"You're perceptive. Tell me about my exceptions, young man."

"If you gave Noella the necklace, you visited a home where not everyone believed in you."

"She was the only one who did. How did I justify it?"

"I have no idea," Tom said.

"I believe she knows."

"She didn't tell me."

"She wrote me that Christmas."

"Even I wrote to Santa when I was—"

"She was old enough to decide for herself, and she chose to believe. Further, her request was not for herself. That is the criterion."

Tom was speechless. Would he remember this?

"I'll show you the jewelry workshop tomorrow," Kris said. "You might even get your hands dirty."

Tom could not stay awake.

SEVENTEEN

Trial by Fire

NOELLA FELT UTTERLY alone. She drifted in and out of
sleep. Never again would she criticize Tom's negativity.
He had been right. Life was not fair. Things did not always turn out the way they should. Noella would never
again be so naive. It was time to grow up.

She stood and stretched. In the cool of the wee
hours Noella extended her arms and longed to draw
them back with Tom in their embrace. Instead she
crossed them over her chest and broke into sobs she
feared would never end. She fell to her knees and felt
she could weep out her very soul.

"Tom," she whispered hoarsely, "I love you, love you,
love you—"

The phone rang. "Walt just called," Rufus said.

"Tom's bag and his belongings were found in the wreckage. Also three bodies, but not Tom's yet."

WHEN TOM AWOKE in the late morning, Mrs. Kringle presented him a wooden crutch. It fitted as if it had been made for him. It had, she said. "The helpers measured you in the night." She left on his bed the clean and dry shoes and clothes he'd worn on the plane. "Breakfast is ready in the kitchen when you are."

Tom gingerly changed out of the gigantic nightshirt. Whatever Kris Kringle and the elves had done to him had dulled the worst of his pain. The bag with the contents of his pockets was on the dresser. He found everything in order. He put his own wallet in his pocket and stored the bag under the bed.

Tom used the crutch to hobble to the kitchen, where every inch of wall was covered with pigeonholes for cooking ingredients and implements. "Kris has been in the shop for hours," Mother said. "He'd like you to join him."

"Any way I can contact the mortal world from here?"

"You'll be back where you belong before you

know it," she said. "Time has not passed there as it seems to here."

After breakfast Mother pointed to a long one-story wooden building with snow-covered latticework on the windows. The miniature men scurried about, filling wheelbarrows from wagons and pushing them into the workshop through a side entrance. Tom hobbled to the front, leaning on his crutch, and peered through the door at Kris, who stood at a long counter on the far wall. The big man waved him in.

The workshop was not what Tom expected. Not a toy was in sight. At one end the miners' entrance featured a short close-set rail track for the wagons. He saw a smelting pot and a busy bunch of helpers transferring the mined material into the furnace, where it was purified, melted, and molded into sheets. These were put on a conveyor belt where more helpers chose the thinnest sheets, used wire cutters to snip them into narrow strips, and sent them in another direction to the chain-making station.

"Surprised?" Kris said, working in half the uniform Tom assumed he wore Christmas Eve: shiny black boots, red satin pants held up by wide red suspenders, and a white undershirt. His red jacket hung on a peg.

His glasses were in place, pipe in his mouth, and he wore a mischievous grin. "Even Santa sweats," he said.

Tom watched as Kris worked with his own cutting tool. The last helper on the supply line labored lightning fast, cutting the sheets into rectangles about the size of business cards. These tumbled off the belt into a metal bowl that jostled them into stacks, straightened them with spring-driven appendages, and delivered them to Kris's bench.

Kris scored each rectangle and bent it in two. Then he trimmed off the four edges with round cuts, leaving a thick circle of platinum. He snipped at the top to leave a spot for the chain, punched a hole in the pendant or embossed it, then held the finished piece over a concentrated flame and filed and wire-brushed it smooth. While it was still soft, he carved a phrase on one side and a birth date on the other. Tom saw no reference list.

"Where do you get the information?" he asked.

"I just know. It's one of the privileges."

"You're making so many. Why don't more people have them?"

"We make thousands. There are billions of you. And don't assume you are the only dimension that exists. You know now there are at least two. Trust me, there are more."

"More dimensions?"

"Not to mention planets."

"You mean?"

"Rule out nothing."

Kris worked so quickly Tom felt as if his brain had been fast-forwarded. When each piece was finished, Kris held it over the flame again long enough to keep it pliable for the next helper, who burnished and polished it and sent it to the chain station.

"Want to try one?" Kris said. "I'll walk you through it."

He selected a shim of platinum from the stack and handed it to Tom, who leaned on his crutch. "Score it," Kris said, giving him a stylus. "Make it straight."

Tom's first attempt failed.

"Not a problem," Kris said. "Score it again. The heat will cover the scars. When it's been through the fire, it will look perfect."

Kris led Tom through the sequence. Tom felt awkward but was pleased with the result.

"Next we punch it or emboss it," Kris said. "Once more through the flame, and I will etch it. I'd let you do that too, but it takes much practice before mortals get it right. Tell you what I will do, however," he said, selecting a pair of tiny letters from a wooden box of type. He fastened the letters together with a small metal clamp. "Those your initials?"

Tom held the mold before his eyes. It read "TD" in reverse. Kris waved the pendant over the flame, then set it backside up before Tom and handed him a mallet. "One sharp strike, and the artiste is identified," he said, holding the letters in place with his fingers.

Tom hesitated.

"Remember," Kris said, "you can't hurt me."

Tom rapped on the mold, and Kris showed him the result. "Almost invisible, but you and I will always know who created this piece. Now the last step before etching." He turned to a helper. "Is this a cut or an emboss?"

"Klodeck," the little man said. Kris handed Tom what looked like an industrial-strength paper punch. Kris held the pendant in it and told Tom to squeeze.

"Put some muscle into it," Kris said.

Tom squeezed with both hands and the platinum gave way with a loud snap. The cutout flew into the air, and a helper deftly caught it. He winked at Tom and put the piece on a belt that took it back to the smelter. "No waste," Kris said.

Tom had punched out the shape of a Christmas tree, just like the one on Noella's pendant. The thought of her made his heart ache.

Kris showed Tom an embossing tool that was similar to the punch. "We heat the piece more for embossing," he said. "This pushes the shape of the tree from the bottom and leaves a perfect relief of it on top."

"Which get punched and which get embossed?"

Kris removed his pipe. "A Fairyland mystery," he said, smiling. "Mortals are told some things. Others they must learn."

Kris replaced his pipe, held Tom's piece close to his eyes, and dug into it with the etcher. He passed the finished pendant to the helper at his left, who began the polishing. "I'll walk you to the door," Kris said, a gentle hand on Tom's shoulder. "The beautiful necklaces begin deep in the ground. It takes work to get to the material and then many steps before it becomes a finished product. It's heated as often as necessary. Imperfections, mistakes"—here he winked—"inaccurate scorings are covered in the trial by fire. The difference between the original ore and the pendant, you must agree, is enchanting."

Tom had interviewed enough people to know when someone finished talking. He was desperate to stay in the presence of this wonderful man in this magical place. "You're not coming back to the house?"

"Sorry," Kris said. "More work to do. And you need your rest."

Tom was suddenly so sleepy he could hardly speak. He forced himself to form words. "Will you be there when I wake up? Will we talk more?"

Kris looked at him knowingly. "Once you've been here, my friend, you'll never be far from me. There's no more need to talk. Only to rest and recover."

"Is this good-bye?"

"It takes two mortals to say good-bye, friend. It's something I never say."

"But will I—"

"Say good-bye, son. And I'll say, 'Sleep well. Awaken even better. And I'll be seeing you.'"

Mrs. Kringle was waiting when Tom reached the house. She opened the door of the guest room, gave him a motherly embrace, and gently took his crutch. Tom limped to the bed and sat atop the fluffy covers. He slowly turned and lay on his stomach, letting his good arm hang off the side of the bed. As he was losing consciousness, he felt for the bag he had stashed under the bed. He gathered the top in his palm and fell asleep.

EIGHTEEN

The Reunion

SOUNDS AND SMELLS told Tom he was no longer in the snow, no longer visiting Santa's complex. He was startled to find himself in an open-backed gown, an IV line in his arm and an ID tag on his wrist. He squinted at it and blinked at a doctor sitting to his left.

"Mr. Douten?" the doctor said, his accent thickly German. "Do you know where you are?"

Tom formed the words laboriously, his mouth cottony. "Wristband says Zwingli, Zurich. Switzerland?"

"Zwingli International. Do you know what happened to you?"

He thought a moment. "Plane crash?"

"And how did you get here?"

Tom shook his head.

"You were discovered at our emergency entrance at six this morning. Your injuries are remarkably minor. Slightly dehydrated, thus the IV. Your leg will be uncomfortable for some time, but you should be ambulatory."

"I can go?"

"German authorities want to ask how you got all the way here from the Black Forest."

"What day is it?" Tom managed.

"Sunday, December twentieth."

"Only Sunday?"

"Any memory of being aided by anyone? Loaded aboard a plane? Delivered here?"

"You wouldn't believe me. I crawled, but—"

"You didn't crawl here. Whoever brought you left you with your belongings. We're assuming you want the victims' effects delivered to their relatives?"

Tom was still in a fog. "The ring is the pilot's; the jewelry is the smaller Canadian's."

"Your good Samaritan apparently wishes to remain anonymous."

"Jus' tell 'em Kris Kringle dropped me here."

The doctor smiled. "You're fine. Extremely fortunate, but fine."

Tom felt better a couple of hours later when he was brought his wallet and a phone. His clothes had been

cleaned in the hospital laundry. He phoned Walt
Mathes's home. The connection was only fair. Mrs.
Mathes answered.

"Gail, it's Tom Douten calling Walt from Switzerland."

"This is not amusing!"

"Please, Gail!"

"Walt, somebody's claiming to be Tom."

"Give me that phone," Walt said. "Who is this?"

"Walt, it's really me! I went down with the plane
and woke up in Zurich, man!"

"If this is a joke—"

"Walt! Listen! Vajde's my hero! Rufus is my buddy!
Noyer is a butt!"

"Thank God, Tom! Are you all right?"

Tom asked Walt to help get him back to the States
as soon as possible. Walt said, "If they dream of holding you, we'll send in the troops!"

"I KNOW YOU'RE there, dear," came Rufus's voice from
Noella's machine. "Don't rush."

"Hey, Rufe," she said wearily.

"Sit down, hon," he said.

"Did they find the body?"

"Tell me you're seated, and I'll tell you the latest."

Rufus was sweet. A bit chauvinistic, but she humored him.

"Okay, I'm sitting."

"Listen carefully, Noella. Tom is alive. He's at a Zurich hosp—"

Noella burst into tears and stood. "Rufus! Don't you dare do this to me unless it's absolutely true!"

"Nobody knows how he got there, but it's him. Walt even talked to him on the phone."

"You're not kidding me? Where is he? I'm going!"

"Slow down, girl. He may already be on his way home."

"How is he? How did he survive?"

"He was pretty banged up, but somehow he got out of there. He'll have to tell us the rest."

"I love you, Rufus. Tell me I'm not dreaming."

"You're not, Noella. Merry Christmas."

Noella and Rufus celebrated in the *Tribune* office, and by Sunday evening the place was hopping with colleagues who had come to see if the news was true.

To her dismay, Noella was told that with the holiday travel crunch, Tom would come home from Zurich through Frankfurt, London, New York, and finally O'Hare. He would pick up seven hours, but with all the connections, he was not expected until midday, Wednesday.

Noella couldn't wait for Tom to know exactly where she was on the Santa issue. She knew he would be pleased.

TOM ARRANGED BY phone to have a laptop computer waiting for him in Frankfurt and on the flight to London disgorged himself of the entire story. He left out Noella's name and her relationship to him, but everything else was included. From a communications center in London he transmitted his copy to the *Tribune*. On his way back to Heathrow he discovered an exclusive shop where he selected three perfect handmade gifts.

Wednesday morning, on the last leg of the trip, he called Walt from the plane. "Any chance of sneaking into O'Hare without a big ballyhoo?"

"Doubt it," Walt said. "Rufus will be there to get you, but your second segment ran this morning, and everybody says the series has Pulitzer written all over it. *Reader's Digest* wants exclusive magazine rights. Most important is that you're still among us, but, man, Tom, that's the best fiction I've seen since 'Yes, Virginia, there *is* a Santa Claus.' We're printing around the clock and already have more requests for copies than of any other piece ever, including the moon landing and all the Bulls' championships. I'm sure there's already a crowd at O'Hare."

Tom wanted to call Noella, but he would wait and talk to her in person. What would she think when she learned he'd been saved by Santa? Nothing stood between them anymore.

NOELLA HAD DEVOURED Tom's account of the necklace-manufacturing process in the *Tribune* Tuesday and Wednesday mornings. She loved Fairyland and the warm and wonderful Mrs. Kringle. What had happened to Tom? What would have inspired not only his first piece of fiction but also a fantasy? He wrote with the same passion as always, including specific, nitty-gritty things that made her feel as if she were there with him.

She knew the details of the jewelry making stemmed from her own necklace. It didn't matter that she had finally concluded it must have come from her father. She loved Tom's series anyway. She couldn't wait to tell him she loved him. It wouldn't be right to plant one on him even before she had a chance to tell him she was withdrawing her belief-in-Santa prerequisite from their engagement. But she would explode if she didn't kiss him soon.

Noella knew they would be unable to talk at O'Hare. Rufus agreed to get Tom back to his apartment quickly and to tell him she would be waiting in the parking lot.

NINETEEN

The Revelation

NEITHER RUFUS NOR Noella counted on the resource-
fulness of the local press. Many guessed Tom would
hightail it home. Noella couldn't park near the place for
all the remote-broadcast trucks and reporters in the lot.

She called Rufus's car phone and left a message.
"Sandburg jammed. Plan B, Round-the-Clock."

RUFUS CASHED IN a few chips with Chicago cops, who
kept an eye on his car, idling at the curb upstairs at
O'Hare. Once Tom had thanked everyone and broken
away from the cameras, Rufus jogged ahead and waited
in the car. He pulled away with Tom before the press
figured out what had happened.

"I'd hug you, Tommy, but I need to drive."

"That's all right," Tom said. "I don't want to hug a big ugly man right now anyway."

Rufus's phone beeped, and he held the receiver to his ear. "Plan B."

Tom felt a tingle up his spine at the prospect of seeing Noella.

NOELLA SAT AT Round-the-Clock, nervous as she had ever been. When Rufus pulled to the curb, she lost all resolve. She ran out as Tom emerged, limping, his face scraped and bruised. Though he carried packages, she kissed him, soft and long.

Rufus lowered his window. "You kids be all right without me?" They ignored him. "All right, then," he said. "Okay. Well. Bye."

TOM JUST WANTED to look at her. "I have so much to tell you," he said.

She covered his mouth with another kiss. "Inside," she said. "I've got things to tell you too, and I can save us some time and grief."

She helped him into the booth, and Rita brought his coffee. "Haven't seen you two for a while," she said. "Hey, what happened to you?"

"Long story," Tom said.

"And it's going to have to wait," Noella said.

"Fair enough." She left them alone.

"Tom," Noella said, "I love you. And I have something for you."

She handed him a small black box. Inside, packed in cotton, was her platinum necklace. Tom looked up at her, puzzled.

"I want you to have it, Tom. Keep it as a memento of when I needed to believe. Now I see that—"

"But you were right, Noe! That so-called fiction in the *Trib* is true. It happened. It really did."

Noella's smile had frozen. "Tom, you don't have to do this. I know now that—"

"I'm telling you the truth, babe. We may become the craziest married couple in history, but we both literally believe in Santa Claus."

"Tom, now, just a minute."

"Noella, I saw these pendants made. I helped Kris make one!"

"I read that."

"You read between the lines, didn't you? You knew, right?"

"Knew?"

"That it was real. I was there, Noella. I met him and the elves; only they don't call them elves, they call them helpers, and—"

"Tom, you're going too fast."

"I made none of it up."

"You believe you were actually in Fairyland with Kris Kringle."

"I even found out how you qualified for your pendant."

"I read that too."

"He knows you. Knows you're a true believer."

THEY HAD SWITCHED ROLES. Noella had grown up, come to her senses, seen herself for the dreamer she was. Couldn't Tom see he had pieced his yarn together from the very issues they'd been through?

"I'm so relieved you're alive," she said. "I know you've been through a horrible ordeal, but you sound the way *I* did when you concluded I was in denial."

"But *I* was in denial, Noella! I was wrong. You were right!"

"So how did Santa blow my birth date?"

"That's not the kind of mistake they make there."

"Really."

IT DAWNED ON TOM that Noella doubted him.

"You're hurting," she said. "Jet-lagged. You need rest."

"I've never been more certain of anything. When I crawled from that wreckage, I told myself I would not let us fall apart over the Santa thing."

"I told myself the same, Tom. You can believe in the Easter Bunny for all I care."

Tom smiled. "But aren't you glad to know you were right?"

Noella gently touched his hands. "I'm grateful to have learned it doesn't matter."

"Keep your necklace until I convince you. I just have to prove this to you," Tom said.

"No," she said. "You don't."

THEY AGREED SHE would spend Christmas Eve with her family, he with his. Then he would join her at her mother's condo for lunch on Christmas Day. Tom left

Noella with the Christmas gifts he had brought for her and her mother and grandmother. She also still had her necklace, and that gave her an idea. The next day, Thursday, December 24, Noella drove to Northwestern for a private meeting with Dr. Joseph Neutz, a professor of geology who had known her father. "I appreciate your seeing me, today of all days," she said.

"Anything for Dr. Wright's girl," he said, smiling.

Noella shortcut the small talk. "Do you have the equipment to evaluate this metal?"

Dr. Neutz pulled thick reading glasses from his pocket and studied the necklace. "Of course you know it's platinum?" he said.

"I suspected."

"It'll take me a few hours."

BEFORE LEAVING FOR the South Side, Tom phoned Noella's mother. "There's something I have to ask," he said. "I need the truth about Noella's necklace. If her father gave it to her, why would the birth date be wrong?"

There was a long silence. Miriam's voice came raspy and labored. "My mother-in-law is the only other living soul who knows this, but I've felt awful about it all Noella's life. My brother took his own life on

Christmas Eve in 1963. Noella was born two years later to the day, and I would not have been able to abide being reminded of the suicide every year on her birthday. As it is, we try to cover the pain by opening one gift on Christmas Eve. We waited a couple of days before telling anyone, then announced Noella had been born the day after Christmas."

Tom felt the hair on the back of his neck. "You thought your husband gave Noella the necklace. Why?"

"We were going through a bad season in our marriage, and I thought he did it to spite me. I'm happy to say we patched things up before his death, and though I gave him many opportunities to admit having done it, he never did. It's always been a mystery to me."

"Don't you think it's time Noella knew about her real birthday?"

"Don't tell her. Please. What possible good could it do now?"

Tom couldn't tell her everything. "It would right a wrong," he said. "You lied to her."

"Only to protect her."

"No disrespect, Mrs. Wright, but it seems you were protecting your own family's reputation."

Tom heard Miriam draw a shaky breath. "If she must know, I need to tell her myself. And I will."

WHEN NOELLA RETURNED that afternoon to retrieve her necklace, Dr. Neutz told her, "This is an extremely pure form of platinum, like nothing I've ever seen. I don't want to belabor this, but platinum is very rare. It makes up only about a millionth of a percent of the earth's core. It costs more than gold."

"Any chance this could have come from Europe?"

"I've never heard of platinum mined in Europe, but neither have I seen anything like this. I would urge you to keep it. I see the date on it, but my guess is that this piece was refined hundreds of years ago. And under supermagnification the etching proves to have been hand carved, obviously by a true artisan."

TWENTY

The Night Before

"Let's open the ones from Tom tonight," her mother said. "I wish he could have come." Noella ached for Tom and looked forward to his joining them the next day.

Rose opened a leather-bound collection of poetry with a card that said, "I can't wait to read some of your favorites to you. Love, Tom."

"That man," Grandmother said. "He knew I would love this. Noella, he's a gem."

Miriam pulled at paper that covered a beautiful metronome. She gasped. "I told Tom I hadn't practiced the piano for ages because my ancient metronome had finally given out. This is handmade!"

Noella missed Santa. While she had come to

her senses about him, at times like this she wished she hadn't. Changing her mind hadn't changed her heart. The little girl in her wanted Santa as part of this Christmas.

She opened Tom's card. "For January through November. Happy birthday. All my love, TD."

Tom had given her an exquisitely tooled jewelry box with "A Visit from St. Nicholas" carved delicately in the top. Noella looked at her mother and grandmother through watery eyes that made the Christmas tree lights dance.

"Excuse me," she said. "I'll see you in the morning."

Noella trudged up to the guest room, changed into her nightgown, and sat on the bed, longing for Tom. She answered a gentle knock. Her mother nervously handed her a sealed envelope. "Don't judge the writing. You and your father were the wordsmiths. It's self-explanatory, and if we don't discuss it, that will be all right with me. I just hope I covered it all." Her mother hurried away.

Noella tore open the envelope and smoothed several handwritten pages on the bed. Her mother had used the fountain pen she loved so much, her last gift from Noella's father.

Dear Noella:

Thirty-five years ago this very day was one of the saddest of my life.

December 24, 1963, was the day my brother, your uncle, died. What you don't know is that he took his own life. . . .

Tom spent the late afternoon and evening at his parents' home, mostly listening to their expressions of relief that he had survived and their laments that Timmy was still in prison. He arrived back at his apartment late and went to bed. He lay on his back, hands behind his head, unable to sleep.

Before he met Noella, Tom had never decorated his apartment for Christmas. Now he sat up, wide-eyed, and wondered if it was too late to find a tree. It wasn't yet midnight. He limped out to a lot on North Avenue and LaSalle and found ridiculously high prices for latecomers. The stand cost more than the tree.

"Do you have ornaments?" Tom asked.

"You kiddin'? This is the first year we've had stands. Popcorn strings work nice. Paper dolls too."

Tom wasn't going to pop corn or cut paper dolls. He hobbled home and filled the stand with water, then attached the tree. It looked anemic until he lifted and shook it to make the branches unfold. Water slopped onto the rug, but the tree looked better.

He situated it under a spotlight and turned off the other lights, then sat at the kitchen table to study it. Who wouldn't laugh at his unadorned tree? He found it beautiful in its simplicity.

Tom couldn't help but remember childhood Christmases on the South Side, where he shared a bedroom with Tim. They were so sure Santa was real that they imagined bells at the corner and footsteps on the roof. Santa would not come until they were asleep, but the harder they tried, the harder it was to lose consciousness. They were not allowed out of their bedroom before seven in the morning. He and Tim checked the time at least forty times one Christmas Eve.

The next Christmas Dad had been on a binge. Gifts were few, and Mom tried to explain. "It's been a tough year. We just don't have much money."

"But Santa," Tom said, "didn't he come?"

"Oh, Thomas," she said, "you don't still believe that, do you?"

"What?"

"Santa's pretend, Tom. You know that, don't you?"

Tom pretended he had known, but the truth was he was shattered. He traced much of his cynicism to that day.

But now he was no longer a cynic. He pulled a notepad from a drawer.

DEAR SANTA:

I haven't written you for years, and I can hardly believe I'm doing it now. Anybody seeing a professional journalist writing a for-real letter to you would call the men in white coats.

But I was with you recently, and I know you exist. I also want something for Christmas. I would appreciate anything you can do to restore Noella's belief in you. If anybody deserves the magic of Christmas, she does.

I'll leave out a few cookies, and I apologize if they're stale. Pass along my greetings to the Mrs., and may you both have a Merry Christmas.

Thanks for everything.

Tom

Tom left the notepad on the counter alongside a bottle of water and a paper plate with six cookies. It would be harder to fall asleep tonight than it had been a quarter century before.

NOELLA'S TEARS SPLATTERED the ink. Her mother closed:

> Waiting two days to announce your birth seemed a minor offense. I apologize for my unwillingness to tell you before now. I have no idea who gave you the necklace with your true birthday on it, but now you know why it caused such havoc.
>
> Regardless of when we celebrate your arrival, never forget that you are the most precious Christmas gift I've ever received. Happy birthday.
>
> Love,
>
> Mother

Noella put the letter back in the envelope and slid it under her pillow. She turned out the light and lay in the darkness. No one in her family would have given her a priceless platinum necklace, hundreds of years old and hand-etched with her actual birth date.

TWENTY-ONE

The Visits

CHRISTMAS MORNING TOM'S eyes popped open at seven. It was still dark. His body was alive with anticipation. How he wished he could share this moment with Noella. He splashed his face with cold water and ran his hands through his hair.

In the living room Tom was met with a sight that made his entire body rigid. The tree was beautifully decorated, every inch a stunning masterpiece of color. He laughed and cried and whooped until he remembered the neighbors and pressed a hand against his mouth. On the counter a half bottle of water and two cookies were left. His note was gone. A new one had been written on the same pad Tom had used.

Dear Thomas,

Merry Christmas. Enjoy the gift I sent home with you, which seemed only appropriate under the circumstances.

Your friend,

KK

He had never wanted so badly to tell anyone anything. It was too early to call Noella. How could he prove he hadn't decorated the tree himself and written his own note? He knew he had dead-bolted the door as usual, but he needed concrete proof Santa had been there. If only he could find the gift! But what gift? His health? Sent home with him? Had Santa slipped something into the cloth bag? All that stuff had been returned to the families of the plane crash victims.

Tom couldn't sit still. He called the *Tribune* and reached a security guard. "Any mail come for me?" he asked.

"You kiddin'? Your desk is piled high. You want me to look through it for something?"

"Thanks anyway. I'm coming down."

Still in her robe, Noella sat in the kitchen with Grandma Rose. She heard her mother upstairs. Miriam insisted on making Noella's bed whenever she visited. She returned looking perturbed. "Time for presents," she said.

"Don't wait for me," Rose said, rising slowly. "I'll get there."

Noella followed her mother into the living room. "Something wrong?"

Miriam shook her head.

"Tell me, Mom. Let's not have anything between us, today of all days."

"I just hoped you'd have read my letter last night."

"I thought you didn't want to talk about it."

"I don't, but you should have read it."

"I did, and I appreciated it more than I can say."

"Noella, I just found it under your pillow. Still sealed."

Noella trotted upstairs.

Tom was wired. Santa had visited him, but he couldn't prove it. He showered and shaved and threw on some clothes. By eight o'clock he had pulled into the parking garage near Tribune Tower. He hurried to his desk and pawed through the stack that had accumulated. Much of the mail was from fans of the Christmas articles the *Tribune* had labeled "A Santasy." There was a lot of junk mail and interoffice memos. But there was also a small, padded Federal Express package from Winnipeg.

Tom tore it open, and a letter dropped out.

DEAR MR. DOUTEN:

On behalf of my children, thank you from the bottom of my heart for your thoughtfulness. I can't tell you what it meant to us, in the midst of our shock and grief, to receive Marc's wallet (with all our pictures inside) and his ID bracelet, which I gave him last Christmas.

I trust you will be back to full health soon. Thanks again, and Merry Christmas.

Sincerely,

Mrs. Marcus Kroeker

P.S. I enclosed one item that did not belong to my husband or his partner. It must have belonged to the pilot.

Tom upended the envelope and into his palm slid a platinum necklace. The phrase read, ". . . a day." The

Christmas tree was embossed rather than cut out, and etched on the back was "Born May 15, 1967."

Tom's birthday.

He looked closely at the initials stamped near the edge. KK.

He ran to his car. A phone call wouldn't do.

Noella found the sealed letter. It made no sense. She tore it open and fanned through the pages. It was the very same letter, but the words that had been smeared by her tears were as clear as when they were written. What could she tell her mother, "Santa has dried my tears"?

She went back down, weak-kneed. "I don't understand it," she said. "I must have sealed it back up. I'm sorry, but I can't go another minute without calling Tom."

"Tom we'll wait for!" Grandmother said.

No answer at his apartment. Where could he be? She called her own machine, in case he had called. The only message was from Rufus. "Robert Taylor asked for your number. I told him I'd have to check with you first. I reminded him it was Christmas."

Noella dug in her purse for her phone directory and dialed. "Mr. Taylor? This is Noella Wr—"

"Miss Wright, I appreciate how you took to my little girl. But I can't let Betsy accept this. It's not appropriate for a—"

"I'm sorry? Accept?"

"This necklace. It's obviously very expensive, and I can't—"

"Mr. Taylor, I didn't send a gift to your daughter. I wish I'd thought to, but—"

"No disrespect, ma'am, but this thing looks just like yours. It even says, 'Forever and . . .' on the front. On the back it's got her birthday, which she doesn't even remember telling you."

"That did not come from me."

He paused. "I'm sorry, but no one else would have given it to her, and it looks just like yours."

"I'd like to see it."

"I'd like you to come and get it."

TOM'S CAR SLID into the driveway at the Wright condo. Noella burst from the front door as he got out. "I've got so much to tell you!" she said.

"Me first!" he said, producing his necklace. "Let me see yours."

Noella pressed her pendant against his, and the embossed tree fitted perfectly into the cutout. With the two making a whole now, the pendant read, "Forever and . . ." on the front with ". . . a day" on the back. Tom and Noella held each other so tight they spun in a circle to keep their balance. They laughed and kissed and twirled some more, and Noella saw her mother and grandmother smiling from the window.

All the way to the South Side they interrupted each other with stories of the morning's enchantment. "You're not going to believe this," Tom said over and over, and Noella assured him, "I'll believe everything you tell me for the rest of my life."

On the Kennedy they ran into a blizzard. Tom slowed and put his arm around Noella, who slid close. "I love this!" he said. "I hope it buries the city! This is the third day of winter already. Where's the stuff been?"

BETSY TAYLOR DIDN'T want to take off her necklace. "You don't have to," Noella told her. "We just want to look at it."

"I prefer she take it off," Mr. Taylor said. "We can't accept it."

"Take that up with Santa," Noella said. "I'm innocent."

"Daddy, please!" Betsy said. "It's the best present I ever got!"

Noella examined it. "Turn it over," Tom whispered.

Stamped along the lower edge on the back, so small most people would miss them, were the letters *TD*.

Epilogue

Tom pulled a few strings so he and Noella could be married the next day. That way they would celebrate their anniversary on December 26, the date on which Noella had celebrated her birthday for thirty-two years.

Sue Beaker was matron of honor.

Rufus Young both gave away the bride and served as best man.

Betsy Taylor served as flower girl, wearing a platinum necklace that matched the bride's.

Gary Noyer mistook Dr. Connie Ng's car for Tom's and affixed four pounds of Limburger cheese to the engine. Dr. Ng has filed suit.